MIA LEE IS WHEELING THROUGH MIDDLE SCHOOL

MIA LEE IS WHEELING THROUGH MIDDLE SCHOOL

Melissa and Eva Shang

Written in collaboration with Amy Cobb
Cover and interior art by Brittany R. Jacobs

To Mom & Dad.
To our backers on Kickstarter, especially Paul Beery and Miriam K. Schwartz.
To the 150,000 strangers who showed incredible kindness to us along our journey.
And to all the girls with disabilities out there, wheeling through middle school:
This book is for you.

Chapter One:
A Rolling Entrance

If I starred in a movie, I wouldn't be some fairy tale Cinderella. Forget Prince Charming. I'd rather be the movie director, directing all the scenes with my giant megaphone, like "Places, everyone!" and "Cut!"—except, you know, in sixth grade and in a wheelchair but just as awesome.

Even if I didn't want to be Cinderella, today I would have really loved to roll up in her sparkly enchanted carriage. The first day of school at Terrywood-Weston Middle School might not be a fancy ball, but it was a pretty humongo deal for an eleven-year-old like me. Luckily, the butterflies bopping around in my stomach took a break when the bus driver pulled up at the front of the school because I spotted my best friend, Caroline Zaler, waiting at the door. She waved at me, jumping up and down, while I rolled my wheelchair up the sidewalk. "Howdy, partner!"

Oh no, I thought.

"Saddle up for your first day of middle school, Mia Lee," Caroline went on. Then she acted like she twirled a lasso and roped me. I'm not kidding.

"Caroline, stop!" I begged before her cowgirl routine got way out of hand. I've heard Caroline make neighing sounds like a horse before, and I knew where this was going.

But there was no stopping Caroline this morning. She pretended to twirl her rope above her head again. "I'm gonna lasso them there clouds," she drawled in her best cowgirl voice.

I couldn't watch. Instead, I sank back in my chair and squeezed my eyes shut. This was probably my fault. Picture second grade. That's when I met Caroline for the very first time on the very first day of school. At recess, we pretended to be cowgirls. We needed something to lasso our imaginary horses, of course. So I got the genius idea to use Caroline's long brown braid for a rope. When I said, "Yee-haw!" and swung Caroline's braid, she giggled. We'd been best friends ever since.

Caroline had ditched wearing braids a long time ago. But every year since second grade, on the first day of school, she always called me "partner" and pretended to be a cowgirl all over again. It was like tradition or something. I didn't mind it before. But that was so elementary school, and this was middle school. Now it was just embarrassing.

"Giddyup!" Caroline said then.

This tradition had to end here—now.

"Whoa!" I said, wheeling my chair right in front of Caroline before the entire school saw her "rodeo." She could thank me later.

Caroline stopped dead in her tracks. "Hey, why did you do that? I was just getting to the best part where I take off on Dude, my fake horse."

"Because it's time to put Dude in the barn and leave him there—forever," I said more gently.

Caroline looked confused. "Huh?"

"Remember how we talked a couple of days ago about us being cool this year?"

"Yeah." Caroline nodded.

"So playing cowgirls in middle school—that's not so cool." I hoped I didn't hurt her feelings.

Caroline dropped the pretend reins she'd been hanging on to. "Sorry. You're right. It's just middle school nerves. I feel all—"

"Bonkers?" I asked, filling in her sentence.

"That's it!" Caroline laughed and stuck out her tongue. Then she made her eyes go all googly.

I smiled and shook my head. Caroline hadn't changed at all over the summer. She had what my mom called "quirks." Like Caroline didn't only dig pretending to be a cowgirl. She was also totally into horses—big time! But she lived in an apartment and couldn't have a real horse of her own. So she decorated her whole room in horses: posters, comforter, and a rug. You name it! And her wardrobe? Same thing. She was even wearing a horse shirt today. Glitzy silver sequins dotted the saddle and sparkled in the sun.

But anyway, I got how Caroline felt about starting middle school. So I told her, "I'm a little nervous, too."

"Really?" Caroline asked.

"No, not really." I shook my head. "I'm *a lot* nervous," I admitted.

Caroline looked relieved that she wasn't the only one.

I mean, who knew what to expect today? Sure, there were tons of books and movies all about middle school, but they centered on mean girls and locker problems. So far, I hadn't seen any girls at Terrywood-Weston who looked too mean. And I definitely didn't have to worry about locker problems, not with Miss Jackson around.

Geez, Louise! I'd completely forgotten about Miss Jackson. But as usual, she wasn't too far behind me.

"It's time to head inside, or you'll be late for morning assembly, Mia," Miss Jackson said, coming over to me then. "Let me push your chair. Okay?"

"Okay," I agreed. "Let's roll."

"You've got it. And hello to you, Caroline." Miss Jackson smiled.

"Hey, Miss J!" Caroline smiled back.

Miss Jackson is my aide. Every morning, she meets me at the bus and helps push me to my classes and stuff. I already knew her from last year when I was a fifth grader at Bellmont Elementary. Out of all of my aides so far, she was my favorite. Miss J was young and cool. And she never looked at me like I was some small, injured animal that she felt sorry for.

Some of my aides thought that just because they were in charge of pushing my wheelchair, they were in charge of my life. But that's not so with Miss Jackson. She didn't just take off pushing me. She always asked first, like just now. I liked to push myself when I could. But I usually couldn't for very long, not with my Charcot-Marie-Tooth disease. I know, it sounds like some dessert on the menu at a fancy restaurant in France, right? But really, it's a form of muscular dystrophy. There's nothing sweet about that. So, basically, with all the big medical words cut out, having Charcot-Marie-Tooth disease means it's hard for me to make my hands and legs do what I want them to do.

Caroline ran on ahead of us. "I'll get the door," she said over her shoulder.

"Thanks!" I called after her.

Then Miss Jackson pushed me inside Terrywood-Weston. While she stopped by Principal Williams's office to get the keys that helped us get into places like the elevator, I pushed myself.

"This is it," I half whispered. Then I took a deep breath and smiled sort of nervously at every kid we passed in the hallway. I was really, really excited about making some new friends this year. Caroline and I wouldn't have all our classes together like before. And that's why we had to act like middle schoolers, not some fifth-grade babies.

Now that we were inside, Caroline didn't seem too nervous. At least not until she launched into full motor-mouth mode.

"Can you believe we're finally in middle school, Mia? I mean, tell me. Can you honestly believe it?"

Um, no, I couldn't believe it. But I didn't actually get to say so because Caroline rushed on about her class schedule.

See? That was another one of Caroline's quirks. When she was superduper nervous, like today. Look out! She couldn't keep her lips zipped. I mean, seriously, she talked even more than me. Trust me, that was a lot. My older sister, Ella, even teased me that someday I'd be the host of my own TV talk show. Was that a compliment, or her way of telling me to shut it because she thought I talked too much? I wasn't sure. But if Ella was right and I ever got into show business, I wasn't so sure it would be one of those boring talk shows. Instead, Ella would write scripts, and I would be a director and shoot my own videos, sort of like we already did with some videos I made and shared online.

Caroline whirled around to say something else, and her backpack nearly wiped out a girl hurrying to the gym for assembly. Luckily, the girl dodged it, but she bumped into my wheelchair instead.

"Sorry!" I began, even though, really, it wasn't my fault.

The girl turned and flashed me a glare. "Watch it, klutz!" she said.

Another girl with her looked ready to page the school nurse. "Are you okay, Angela?"

Seriously? She didn't bump me that hard. I mean, I've had worse paper-cut injuries. And wait a sec. Angela? I knew her from somewhere. She looked like one of those girls who posted makeup tutorials online—tons of mascara. I'd already seen lots of new faces today, so I couldn't remember where I'd seen hers before.

"But you were th—" I started to tell Angela she was the one who bumped into me, but she and her friend took off.

"Well, they were rude!" Caroline said.

"Caroline," I said, "I think we just met our first real-life middle school mean girls."

"And they didn't even look that mean."

Caroline was right. They didn't look mean. They looked like walking, talking dolls—the kind of girls that everyone wouldn't mind looking like, even me. And those were the worst kind of mean girls. They looked nice—long eyelashes and cute clothes. But inside, they were pure evil. I shivered. It was a big school, though. I probably wouldn't see Angela again.

But just in case, I saved a few notes in my brain about Angela:

Subject: Possible Mean Girl

Hair: Wavy blonde

Outfit: Logo T-shirt, paired with ripped jeans and tall boots

Note: Excessive use of mascara, lip gloss, and sarcasm

Still Unknown: How is blinking even possible with so much mascara? And Angela didn't even know me, but she already didn't like me. Why?

Because I can't get up and move around a lot, I pay close attention to stuff that most people don't. It's like this bonus app automatically uploaded in my head to store information. I call this info my Brain Files. When I get new details about people or about stuff I want to remember, I just plug them into my brain. That way, I don't forget.

But I couldn't think about Angela anymore right now. I had my very first middle school assembly to go to.

Because I couldn't exactly climb the gym bleachers, Miss Jackson helped me grab a seat on the bottom row next to Caroline. First, we sat through a bunch of staff introductions and school policies. Boring!

But I sat up a little straighter when leaders from different clubs spoke. Besides making new friends, I'd hoped to join some new groups. The first few clubs were not for me, though. One teacher filled us in on Jump In, a jump-roping club. That sounded cool. But a jump rope plus leg braces equaled disaster. There was also the *T-W Middle Times*. Writing for the school newspaper was so not for me.

Then this other teacher spoke into the mic. "Good morning. I'm Mr. Postin. Besides teaching math, I'm also the Video Production Club leader." He smiled. "In VP Club, technology and creativity collide when students learn the basics of movie editing and sound effects. At the end of the school year, we hold a film festival, where students get to show off the movies they made to the whole school. If you're interested in learning more, stop by room one seventeen after school today."

Seriously? I nudged Caroline and whispered, "I think I just found my club."

"That would probably help with your stop-motion videos," Caroline whispered back and smiled.

I smiled, too, because I was really into making videos, especially stop-motion videos. Stop-motion videos are where you keep your camera steady and take a bunch of pictures that are just the teensy tiniest bit different. I usually put my favorite doll, Saige, in the garden and come up with ways for her to act out the story lines Ella writes. Then once I edit the pictures together, it looks like Saige is actually moving around and acting out a scene like a real actress.

I don't have a super fancy video camera or anything. I just use my phone. I posted my first-ever stop-motion video online this summer. It got almost four hundred likes, which is a pretty big deal. So, yeah, I'm really into making movies.

Middle school and VP Club were going to be great. I already decided things would be different at school this year. *I* would be different. If anybody looked at me, wondering why my hands and legs didn't work like theirs, I wasn't going to look away or pretend I didn't see them staring at me like I used to. Nope, not anymore. I was going to look them in the eye and smile. So watch out, T-W Middle. Here comes the new supercool Mia Lee.

Chapter Two:
Super Klutz

I spent the whole rest of the day looking forward to math class in room 117. It was one of the only classes Caroline and I had together, plus Mr. Postin was my teacher. As soon as math was finished, we'd have our first Video Production Club meeting. I could hardly wait!

I held on to the edge of my desk and slid into my seat.

"I'll be right back here, Mia." Miss Jackson pointed to the back of the room.

That was another thing I liked about Miss J. She didn't fuss over me. In class, she always moved my wheelchair out of the way, almost like it disappeared. Too bad my leg braces wouldn't vanish, too. I looked down at them and closed my eyes, wishing they would.

"Wake up, sleepy head." Caroline tapped my arm.

"Don't worry. I'm awake," I said, opening my eyes.

Nope. The braces were still there. I'd gotten new ones over the summer. They were made of the same hard plastic, molded to the shape of my calves, like my old ones. But these had purple Velcro straps and pink hearts on the back. When I wore them, I could hold on to stuff and walk around a little if I went real slowly. So because the braces helped me, they weren't going anywhere.

Apparently, Angela the mean girl wasn't going anywhere either. Just as the bell rang, she plopped into the desk in front of me. The girl she'd been with in the hall earlier before morning assembly sat across the aisle. I'd found out her name was Jess. I had a few classes with both of them today. But luckily, there were no more run-ins between Angela and my wheelchair.

"Welcome to math, your last class of the day," Mr. Postin announced. "You've survived your first day of middle school. But can you survive my math class?"

"Probably not," Caroline whispered, glancing my way.

I smiled. Math wasn't Caroline's thing. It was English. She was always scribbling away in her journal. Sometimes she wrote poems, short stories, or some cartoon we'd come up with. Because I can't hold a pencil for very long at a time, I came up with the cartoon ideas, and Caroline wrote them down.

But math *was* my thing. At my old school, I was the first kid in class to memorize the entire multiplication table from one to twelve. Solving problems made sense to me. First, line up the facts. Then follow the signs until you get the right answer. Easy.

"Let's begin with a fun math project," Mr. Postin said, then grabbed a marker and wrote *Numbers + Fun = Math Scavenger Hunt*. His white hair matched the giant dry erase board hanging at the front of the room. Mr. Postin reminded me of a sweet, old grandpa. I liked him already.

I liked the scavenger hunt assignment, too. We had the rest of the week to find a whole list of different numbers, stuff like a prime number, a fraction, and a number written with a degree symbol. When we found something on our list, we were supposed to take a picture of it with our phone. We could take the picture anywhere—at school, a store, or whatever. That part didn't matter as long as we took the picture ourselves. Whoever found everything on the list first was the winner.

"To make it even more fun," Mr. Postin added, "you'll have a partner to help you find each item on your list. And you *have* to work together to complete the scavenger hunt. Otherwise, you'll be disqualified."

Caroline and I looked at each other and smiled. Both of us knew we'd pick each other for our partner. We'd make a great team, just like always.

"Madison, your partner is Gabe. Taylor, you partner with Jess," Mr. Postin said.

Uh-oh. He was assigning partners. We didn't get to pick our own.

"Caroline, you and Sheldon work together. And Mia, how about you and—" Mr. Postin paused. Then he looked straight at Angela.

Not Angela. Puh-lease not Angela. I sent Mr. Postin a silent message, hoping he'd get it.

Apparently, he didn't.

"Mia, how about you and Angela pair up?" Mr. Postin said.

No! How about me and anybody but *Angela pair up?* I thought. But then, another thought flashed across my brain. This could actually be a good thing. I've seen movies where ordinary girls, like me, became friends with the popular girls, like Angela. And it always started with one little school project.

I could see it all now: Angela and I work together on this scavenger hunt. Then I say something really funny because, you know, I do that all the time. Angela laughs and tells me I'm pretty cool. Then bam! We're like insta-friends. Maybe Mr. Postin was a real genius for assigning Angela to be my partner!

But when Angela turned around in her seat, she didn't look too happy. She even gave me a mean look, like it was my fault Mr. Postin chose me to be her partner.

I tried smiling at Angela, you know, thinking she'd see that I'm nice. And who knows? Maybe Angela was actually nice, too, and not a real mean girl. Maybe the problem earlier was that we were both nervous because of it being our first day at a new school. What if this whole thing with Angela was all just one giant misunderstanding? I mean, it *was* possible, right? But then Angela whirled back around in her seat. She did not smile back. Our insta-friendship was not off to a good start.

After everyone had been assigned a scavenger hunt partner, Mr. Postin said, "Now, let's begin today's lesson with a review of multiplying decimals." He wrote some problems on the board. When his big belly brushed against the board and erased like half of the numbers he'd just written, everyone laughed, even Mr. Postin.

A few minutes later, the class was laughing again. Only this time, they weren't laughing at Mr. Postin.

"Be sure to put your name at the top," Mr. Postin said, passing out worksheets.

I did. At least, I tried. I gave my hands a pep talk. "C'mon, hands. You can do it," I whispered. As usual, they totally ignored me. Somewhere between the "Mi" and the "a" in Mia, my pencil tumbled right out of my hand. That happens sometimes because of my muscular dystrophy. So much for supercool Mia.

Anyway, the eraser must've hit the floor because my pencil bounced up in the air. I shifted in my seat, trying to catch it. Instead, I knocked over my math book. *Thump!* It landed right on top of Angela's purse.

"Wow, you're a real superhero," Angela said, turning to look at me.

"I, uh, I am?" *What was she talking about?* I wondered.

"Sure." Angela smiled. "Super Klutz!"

So then everyone sitting around us who heard Angela busted their guts laughing.

Geez, Louise! I really was wrong about Angela because she wasn't just an ordinary mean girl. She was a middle school monster. Right about now, I wished I really was a superhero. That way, my mask would hide my red cheeks.

"Is everything okay?" Mr. Postin asked, peering over the rims of his glasses.

"Just fine." I nodded. I mean, I had to say everything was fine, even if things didn't really feel so fine. I didn't want to make an even bigger deal out of what just happened.

Caroline had been my best friend long enough to know that my hands didn't work like other people's. It was like, no matter how much I told my fingers to do something, they refused to cooperate. Other kids in class didn't know that yet, but I had a feeling they were already starting to figure it out.

Caroline grabbed my pencil and math book, and she put them back on my desk.

"Thanks," I whispered.

"You're welcome," she whispered back. Then Caroline held up a paper for me to see. She'd drawn a circle, with two dots for eyes and a frowny face. I knew she felt bad about what had just happened.

"It's okay," I mouthed, and I meant it.

Hey, that stuff with Angela, it didn't really matter. What Mr. Postin said at the beginning of class about surviving our first day of middle school was true. I did it! Even if I didn't make a ton of new friends today like I'd hoped, Caroline was still my best friend. Middle school hadn't changed her one bit, thank goodness! And I was still excited about the Video Production Club.

As soon as math class ended, students filed from the classroom. I hoped Angela would leave, too, but no such luck. She didn't budge from the seat in front of me. Caroline stayed behind, too—not because she was joining the club, but you know, to hang out with me.

When the other students coming in were settled in their seats, Mr. Postin began the meeting. "I'm happy so many of you are interested in Video Production Club. Let me show you what it's all about," he said, dimming the lights.

Then he put on a video for us to watch. Clips flashed on the screen of mini-movies that kids had made in the last few years. There was a documentary about the soccer team, a movie about someone's dog, and even a movie that looked like it was supposed to be scary! Most of them were pretty good, too.

When it was over, Mr. Postin said, "Are any of you interested in joining?"

"I am!" I blurted out.

"Great, Mia." The corners of Mr. Postin's eyes crinkled when he smiled. "Anyone else?"

More hands went up across the room, including a hand with perfectly pink polished nails right in front of me—Angela.

I hoped Angela's hand shot up because she was about to ask for a bathroom hall pass, or she just remembered she was in the wrong school. Or better yet, she'd crash landed on the wrong planet and needed directions back to Mars.

"How do we join?" Angela asked.

My brain screamed, *No! Don't tell her, Mr. Postin!*

But he did anyway. "It's simple. Sign up! We also elect club officers," Mr. Postin said. "Anyone running for president must create campaign posters and submit a campaign video. Points earned for campaign videos *and* fellow club members' votes will decide the winner."

"How do we get points for our campaign videos?" I asked.

"I never tell students how points are awarded," Mr. Postin said.

"What? Why?" Someone else asked.

Mr. Postin held up his hands. "I don't want you to become focused on earning specific points. Instead, focus on creating your best work." He added, "VP Club election day is in two weeks."

Two weeks? That wasn't that far off. But I could already picture that official title in our T-W Middle yearbook. Mia Lee, Video Production Club president. Nice. My videos would be so good that they wouldn't just get four hundred likes—they would get four thousand.

Mr. Postin held up some papers. "Here are the rules, if anyone is interested in running for club president. In the meantime, I'll pass around the sign-up sheet."

It didn't take long for the sheet to get to Angela. When she swung around in her seat to pass it to me, I said, "Do I know you from somewhere?"

"I doubt it." Angela frowned. Then she said, "You're crazy if you even think about running for VP Club president. Trust me, you'll just embarrass yourself."

"Yeah," Jess chimed in. "Angela will win. And you'll lose. I guarantee it!"

Then they both strutted off like supermodels on a runway.

After the meeting, Caroline stopped by my locker. "Don't pay any attention to Angela and Jess. You should totally run for VP Club president, Mia."

"I dunno." I picked at a loose thread on my wheelchair seat. "Angela's probably right. I mean, why embarrass myself by losing the election?"

"Oh, come on!" Caroline said. "I think you're the coolest girl in school." She smiled then. "So don't lose the election. Win it!"

That sounded good. But how?

Caroline looked like she knew. "Mia, you just need to find out who last year's club president was. Then you can ask how he or she won, like what kind of video he or she made and stuff," she rushed on. "And then this year, *you'll* win. Got it?"

"Got it!" I said. That sounded like a great plan. "All we gotta do is get last year's yearbook to look up the president."

"Exactly. Then you'll figure out how to win the election," Caroline said.

Caroline made winning the election seem super easy. Her plan just might work.

Chapter Three: Breaking The News

"See you tomorrow, Mia," Miss Jackson said, helping me down the steps of the special needs bus after the Video Production Club meeting that afternoon.

"Same time? Same place?" I joked. Because, of course, Miss J would be here again in the morning to help me get to school.

"You got it!" Miss Jackson said. Then she waved right before the bus pulled away from the curb in front of our red brick townhouse.

Since my backpack was too heavy for me to lug inside by myself, Mom was there to meet me as soon as I got off the bus. "Hi, Mia! How was your first day of middle school?"

But I couldn't answer just then because Mom wrapped me in a giant bear hug. My lips were smooshed against her shoulder. I breathed in the familiar lavender-scented perfume that Mom always wore. It'd been her favorite perfume for as long as I could remember. Dad bought it for her when they first got married, and she said wearing that perfume reminded her of him. And now that Dad worked at a college in Beijing, we didn't get to see him a lot, except during breaks for Thanksgiving, Christmas, or summer. We did video chats, of course, and lots of them.

Anyway, Mom helped me to the wooden ramp that she and Dad had a construction crew build for me a few years ago. I could walk a little if I had something to hang on to. Holding on to the handrails made it easier for me to walk to our front door.

"So, tell me, Mia. How was your first day of school?" Mom asked again when we were in the dining room.

"Not bad," I said, settling into a chair at the table. Now that it was all over, it really mostly wasn't that bad, except for the stuff with mean girl Angela. Still, it felt really good to be home. Home was safe. Nobody stared at me here. I could just be myself, you know, normal, or at least normal for me.

Mom began unpacking my backpack. Then she spread all of my books and binders across the table in front of me, so I could reach them easier.

"Do you have a lot of homework?" Mom asked.

"I have a ton of reading in science, a map study on western Europe, and some math problems," I said.

"You get started on your homework while I get started on supper." Then Mom disappeared into the kitchen.

I just spent the whole day at school. I wasn't ready for homework, not yet. First, I watched a few stop-motion videos online. Then I reached for my phone.

Mia Lee: Hey, Ella!

A few seconds later, my phone chimed the first few beats of my favorite pop song. It was the special text tone I'd set for Ella when she went to college. That way, as soon as she texted, I always knew it was her.

Ella Lee: Hey! What's up?

Mia Lee: Tons of stuff!

I told Ella all about my first day of school, how mean Angela was, and that she was my assigned partner for Mr. Postin's math scavenger hunt. I finished by telling Ella all about the VP Club election.

Ella Lee: That sounds cool! But what about Mom?

Mia Lee: What about her?

Ella Lee: Do you think Mom will let you run?

Mia Lee: I dunno.

I hadn't thought about it before, but Ella was right. Sometimes Mom could be a little overprotective. She wasn't really like that with Ella, though. Good thing, too, or else Ella would never have gone away to college last fall. But Mom worried about me a lot because of my disability. So she might not go for letting me even join the VP Club, much less run for club president.

"Mia, time to wash up. Supper is ready," Mom called from the kitchen.

Mia Lee: Gotta go, Ella. Talk soon!

By the time I washed my hands, Mom already had supper on the table—rice, sautéed vegetables, and beef stew steamed from my plate. I stuck out my tongue and pretended to gag.

"Mia!" Mom said, but I saw her trying to hide a smile.

"Just kidding, Mom."

She laughed then. "Yeah, right."

Mom knew I really wasn't kidding. That's because this was *not* my favorite meal, and she knew that, too. But Mom and I had a deal. We ate more traditional Chinese-style foods during the week. On the weekends, I got to pick what I liked—tacos, hot dogs, chicken nuggets. Fair enough.

While Mom was laughing, it seemed like the perfect time to talk about VP Club. I couldn't just spring it on her, though. I had to be smooth about it. As I pushed snow peas around on my plate with my spoon, I started talking about school again.

"So I got this cool math assignment today," I said, filling Mom in on the scavenger hunt.

"That does sound like fun." She squeezed lemon into her water. "Have you found any numbers on your list yet?"

I shook my head. "No, not yet. See, I have a partner. Mr. Postin said we have to find everything on our scavenger hunt list together."

"Is Caroline your partner?"

"Nope," I said.

Mom looked surprised.

"She would have been, but Mr. Postin assigned us partners," I explained. "So my partner is Angela."

"Who?" Mom said.

"Angela Vanover. She's this superpopular girl with like perfect hair and makeup and clothes." Basically, everything about Angela was pretty much amazing. Not that I was jealous or anything.

Mom wiped her mouth on her napkin. "I don't think I know her."

The way Angela acted today, I wished I didn't know her either, but I didn't tell Mom that. I never told her when somebody was mean to me or whatever. She'd only worry more. Then if she worried more, she'd hover more. And if she hovered more, then I didn't get any space to do stuff on my own—not good.

So I got off the topic of Angela real quick and bounced it back to school instead. "Yeah, I think I found a club I'd like to join this year."

"Oh?" Mom leaned forward in her seat. "What kind of club? I remember Ella joined a book club in middle school. There was a book exchange each week, and Ella loved it. That would be perfect for you, Mia."

"It's not a book club," I said.

"Is it the school newspaper? You know, Ella was the editor of the school newspaper in middle school, too. Remember the year she won that junior journalist award?" Mom smiled.

See, Mom thinks being a good writer means that you're smart. She used to win all these essay contest when she was younger, and Ella also won a bunch of essay contests. But writing is Ella's thing, not mine. Mom just didn't get how cool stop-motion videos really were. I think making movies makes you just as smart as writing essays.

"And," Mom went on, "I'm sure you have a story hiding inside of you that's waiting to get out, Mia."

I wanted to pretend to look around then, like in the bend of my elbow or underneath my ponytail and say, "Nope. No stories are hiding inside of me!" But I knew Mom wouldn't think that was too funny. Instead, I said, "It's not a writing club either. It's the VP Club."

"VP Club?" Mom repeated. "What's that?"

"Video Production Club. The club would really help me with my video-making skills. Then my stop-motion videos would probably get even more likes."

Mom wasn't smiling now. She frowned. "Don't you think this video quirk of yours is getting over the top, Mia?" she said. "First, you post videos on the Internet for everyone to see. And now joining this club, too?"

"I don't want to just join the VP Club, Mom." I figured I may as well go ahead and drop bomb number two on her now, too. "I'm going to run for club president."

The lacy table cloth in front of Mom swayed back and forth then. Even though I couldn't see her hands under the table, I knew Mom was twisting her fingers together. She always did that when she got upset about something. My posting videos online definitely made Mom upset. She hadn't exactly caught on to social media like the billions of other people on this planet yet.

"I don't know about this video club, Mia," Mom finally said. "I think you should at least consider a book club or the school newspaper. Besides, running for a club office involves a lot of work. I'm afraid it would be too tiring for you."

That's another thing that bugged me. People thought my disability made me tired all the time. It didn't. I mean, hello! I'm the one who owns this disability. I know when I'm tired and when I'm not. "Making videos does not make me tired," I finally said.

I dropped the whole VP Club thing after that. Instead, I focused on spooning up some carrots. I threaded the spoon through my fingers on one hand. Then I used my other hand to keep it steady, so it didn't fall out. I was really careful. However, when my spoon was almost to my lips, it slipped. The spoon clattered on the table, and carrots flew everywhere.

"Here, let me help you!" Mom rushed to grab my spoon.

"I've got this, Mom," I said, grabbing the spoon before she could. I didn't want to hurt her feelings, but there was so much stuff I couldn't do for myself, like even putting toothpaste on my own toothbrush. When I *could* do something for myself, I wanted to do it, even if that meant I made a mess sometimes.

Mom said in Chinese, "Do you really think you can win the election, Mia?"

I think that was Mom's way of pointing out that I couldn't always do things like some people, even easy things like feeding myself. I mean, holding my own spoon was hard for me. So how could I do something like win a club election? I got it. Mom was worried about me running in the election because she loved me, and she didn't want me to get hurt if I lost. I also knew she was right. Winning the election wouldn't be easy.

Anyway, even though I understood Chinese, I didn't speak it very well. So I answered Mom back in English. "Yes, I do think I can win!"

Mom stood up and smiled again then. "You've always been sassy, Mia, like me when I was a girl." She kissed the top of my head. "Join the VP Club. But if this election makes you too tired, you have to withdraw. Deal?"

I didn't feel like arguing anymore. "Deal," I said.

Mom started clearing the table after that. And I reached for my science book to begin reading "Chapter One: Amazing Atoms." Yawn!

I'd read only a few paragraphs when I got a text from Ella.

Ella Lee: So did you talk to Mom yet?

Mia Lee: Yep! Just now.

Ella Lee: And???

Mia Lee: And it went OK. I'm still alive! Lol!

Then Ella texted back *True!* and a smiley face.

I tried to go back to reading about protons, neutrons, and electrons after that, but I couldn't stop thinking about the VP Club. Being elected club president would be the coolest thing ever if I could pull it off. But how did I even begin my campaign? I'd never done one before.

Then I remembered Caroline's Video Production Club president plan. She and I would meet in the school library tomorrow to find last year's T-W Middle yearbook. When I found out who the won the VP Club election last year, I could get some ideas to help me win the VP Club election this year.

Then I'd show Mom that making videos wasn't just some quirk. And I'd show Angela that I wasn't a Super Klutz. I was super serious competition! I'd prove it to everybody—starting tomorrow.

Chapter Four: Act Like A Middle Schooler?

But the next day in the library, I found out talking to last year's Video Production Club president wasn't going to be so easy after all. When I showed Mrs. Wheatley, the school librarian, the club president's yearbook picture, she said, "Dalton was a good kid. We were sad to see him go."

"Go? You mean like he switched schools?" I asked.

"Oh no, dear." Mrs. Wheatley shook her head. "He switched states. Dalton moved to Idaho."

"That's terrible news," Caroline said.

I scrunched up my nose. "Do people even live in Idaho?" I joked.

Caroline and Mrs. Wheatley both laughed. Yeah, it was funny. But now our plans to get some tips from Dalton to help me win the VP Club election were squashed. That wasn't so funny.

"So now what?" I asked Caroline after we'd thanked Mrs. Wheatley and we were out in the hallway.

She shrugged. "I'm not sure. But don't worry. You'll figure something out," Caroline called as she hurried off to science class.

I'd have to figure it out a lot later because then Miss Jackson pushed me into the elevator and up to the second floor to the classroom of doom, otherwise known as English class. Me and English, we didn't exactly get along. I mean, I speak it perfectly. No problem there. But when it came to writing actual words, forget it. Ella was the writer in our family.

So far, my writing skills seemed to be delayed—permanently. Blank notebook pages made me freeze. Blinking computer cursors hypnotized me or something. When I finally started a paragraph, too many thoughts raced through my brain all at the same time. Then my ideas got all jumbled up.

We'd almost made it to room 220 when I said, "My English book! It's still in my locker."

"No problem," Miss Jackson said. "Wheel yourself into class, and I'll grab your book."

"Thanks! My combination is 94–28—"

Before I could finish, Miss Jackson put her finger to her lips to shush me. "Don't tell anyone your combination, Mia. Other kids might overhear and try to break into your locker."

Puh-lease. Grown-ups worried about weird stuff sometimes. I mean, so far, nobody at T-W Middle looked like a locker burglar to me. I almost laughed picturing some kid tiptoeing up and down the hallway, sneaking into all the lockers. Still, I didn't want to hurt Miss J's feelings.

Miss Jackson held up the red lanyard she wore around her neck. "Besides, I have a locker key right here." She jingled the keys. "Along with almost every other key used in the school."

"Prepared Miss Jackson—as usual," I teased. Really, I was glad she was prepared. When Miss J was around, I didn't have to worry about trying to make my fingers spin the dial.

Miss Jackson smiled and told me to hurry on to class. So I did.

"Mia! Mia! Over here!" Someone waved from the back of the room.

Wait, I knew that girl. It was Rory Thomas. She went to Bellmont Elementary last year, too. Some kids secretly called Rory a teacher's pet, but I liked her. She helped push my wheelchair sometimes. I also liked Rory's round pink cheeks. They reminded me of my doll Saige.

"Hey, Rory!" I smiled and waved back.

"Do you want to sit with me?" Rory asked when I wheeled myself over.

"Sure!" I said. When I grabbed a seat beside Rory, it felt like things were sort of looking up. Yesterday, almost all of the seats were taken by the time I got to class, and I sat with some kids I didn't even know.

Rory glanced at my folder. "Nice jellyfish."

Told you I can't draw. That wasn't a jellyfish. It was Angela, all morphed into a monster. That's why I gave it shaggy hair and extra-sharp, pointy teeth. I even called it the Mean Middle School Monster. Hey, that would make a funny cartoon! I couldn't wait to tell Caroline my newest idea. She'd love it.

Cartoons would have to wait, though. Ms. Randells was starting class. She was young, with curly blond hair, and wore a big, blue scarf tied around her neck. Based on the number of grammar posters she had hanging around her classroom, I could tell that she really—and I mean *really*—loved verbs.

"As I told you yesterday, we're going to learn a lot about grammar this year," Ms. Randells began. "And you'll master the mechanics of language by writing—daily." She smiled, as if she'd just given us all a big fat present.

Writing every day? Seriously? Ugh!

"In fact," Ms. Randells said, tugging her scarf over her head and plopping it on her desk, "we'll begin right now." But then she fluffed her hair back into place and frowned. "Just a moment, class. I seem to have misplaced an earring."

Ms. Randells searched all around the room, like it was a game of hide-and-seek, and she was "it."

"Maybe it got hooked onto your scarf when you took it off," I finally said.

When Ms. Randells checked there, she held up the earring and smiled. "It did. Thank you, Mia."

"How did you guess that?" whispered Rory.

I shrugged. "I just noticed her scarf was big and billowy, perfect for an earring to plop on." I didn't tell Rory this because she probably wouldn't understand, but I was just good at picking up on details that most people don't even notice. It was part of my Brain Files app, I guess.

Then Ms. Randells passed out worksheets and told us to brainstorm and jot down a bunch of stuff about ourselves like our talents, our hobbies, or anything interesting. We were supposed to turn it into an essay so that she could get to know us better. She told us to have fun, right before she asked Miss Jackson to help her make some extra copies. They both stepped out of the room.

Have fun? Yeah, right. I stared at my page. This was it. The part where I totally freeze.

But with Ms. Randells away, the room exploded. Kaboom! Kids jumped out of their seats. Some even jumped *in* their seats. Who could brainstorm with this much noise?

I glanced over at Rory.

"Ms. Randells will not be happy," she said. "Maybe I should tell them to knock it off."

"Except we don't know a lot of these kids yet," I reminded her. "So they probably won't listen anyway."

Rory nodded. "Probably not. I just wish people followed the rules more, you know?"

I hid a smile because I knew Rory's inner teacher's pet was doing some serious squirming.

"Let's just do our worksheet," Rory suggested.

"Good idea," I said. Maybe Rory was on to something. Getting on the teacher's good side couldn't hurt.

I managed to write my name and that I'm eleven years old, but I couldn't think of another thing to say after that. It was hard to think when the noise level in this room was about ten seconds from blasting the roof right off.

I checked to see how far along Rory was with her sheet. She wasn't working either. Instead, she stared toward the front of the room. "That doesn't look good," she said.

"What doesn't?" I asked, twisting in my seat for a better look.

"That." Rory pointed to a group of boys hanging out around Ms. Randells's desk. I recognized only one of them from my old school. One boy jabbed his elbow in another boy's chest, like he'd just told some great joke. Then they all laughed like he was the world's funniest comedian.

In the middle of the boys was a girl. She wasn't laughing at all. I hadn't seen her around before. Her black hair was tied with a yellow scarf into a side ponytail. She wore black sweatpants and a T-shirt with some TV show character on the front. I'm not some fashionista, but I knew this girl's clothes weren't exactly featured in one of those glossy teen magazines.

I knew I had to gather some intelligence on the enemy. It took only a second to log a Brain File.

Subject: Boy Bullies

Appearance: Mean

Behavior: Mean

Criminal Activity: Being extra mean in English class

Then I got an idea. "I think the boys are picking on her because of her clothes," I said.

"I think so, too," Rory agreed.

That's when I did something I'd never done before in my whole life. Even Miss Jackson wouldn't be prepared for this. Without even thinking, I stood up and held on to each desk in front of me and slowly made my way to the front of the room, to the circle of boys.

"What's up?" I asked them.

The boys looked surprised at first, but the one I knew from Bellmont spoke up. "What's it to you, Mia?"

"If you're picking on her, it's not cool." Geez, Louise! Was that voice coming out of my face? That girl sounded strong. And right now, I didn't feel so strong.

Another boy stared down his bully nose at me, like he was the leader, a real Mr. McBully. He flashed puppy-dog eyes at me, acting all innocent. "Would we do that?" he asked.

Then they all busted out laughing again.

I glanced over at the girl. She looked relieved that she wasn't the center of attention right now. "Yeah, you would," I said. "But not anymore. So leave her alone."

"Want us to pick on you instead?" the third boy asked.

"You don't want to mess with Mia." Rory came up beside me then. She folded her arms across her chest. "She knows martial arts, you know."

"Sure, she does," Mr. McBully said, looking at my legs.

I knew he was checking out my leg braces. "Yeah, these look bad," I said, holding up one leg. "But you should see the kid who messed with me."

"Whatever," Mr. McBully said.

"You're no fun," the boy from Bellmont said.

I knew we'd gotten our bluff in on them because they all split. I breathed a sigh of relief. I mean, it's not like I stand up to bullies every day.

"Mia"—Rory held her hand up for a high five—"you were awesome!"

"Thanks! So were you," I said, smacking her hand.

"You both were," the girl whom the boys had picked on said. "Thank you so much!"

"You're welcome," Rory and I said together.

"So what's your name?" I asked the girl.

"Daniela Rodriguez," she said. "What's yours?"

"I'm Mia Lee. This is my friend, Rory Thomas."

Daniela smiled and glanced down at her shirt. "I guess nobody around here watches *Doctor Who*, so those boys thought my shirt was a big joke."

I was right. They were making fun of her clothes. Honestly, I'd never watched *Doctor Who* either. "So what's it about?" I asked.

Daniela explained that it was a British show about this time-travelling alien doctor who goes around time and space in a thing called a Tardis.

"Oh, cool," I said.

"Yeah." Daniela nodded. "You should both come over to my house to check it out some time."

"Sounds fun," Rory said.

By now, everybody was pretty much back in their seats. They all stared at us, like we'd just performed some Broadway play. I usually didn't like an audience, but this time, it was different. It felt good to help somebody. It felt good to make a new friend, too. So I didn't care.

That is, until Ms. Randells flung open the door. "Girls, return to your seats. Now!" She yelled, slamming the stack of papers she held onto her desk.

Ms. Randells didn't seem like a yelling sort of teacher. Boy, was I wrong. She may have smiled at me when I helped her find her missing earring earlier, but she definitely wasn't smiling now.

"This is middle school, so act like middle schoolers!" she went on. "Understood?"

I totally understood the part about returning to our seats and the part about this being middle school. But the part about *acting* like middle schoolers? Forget it. I didn't understand that.

How come some middle schoolers were nice, like Rory and Daniela? But then some weren't so nice, like Angela? And like Mr. McBully and those other boys picking on Daniela just now? It didn't make sense. I wasn't sure I'd ever figure middle school out.

Chapter Five:
The Race Gets Real

My stomach already figured out it was lunchtime, though. It rumbled the whole time Miss Jackson pushed me toward the cafeteria. We were nearly there when we almost collided with someone rounding a corner in the hallway. Lucky for her, she jumped out of the way, just in time. Unlucky for me, it was Angela. As usual, Jess was with her.

"Mia, there you are!" Angela said. She didn't look mad, not like she had yesterday when she bumped into my wheelchair. Still, I couldn't believe out of all the kids at T-W Middle, for the second day in a row, Angela had met my wheelchair up close and personal.

Technically, it was Angela and Jess's fault that we almost crashed just now. They were walking on the wrong side of the hallway. Didn't people get that walking down hallways or grocery store aisles was like driving a car? Stay on the right side, people. I didn't want to stick around to listen to Angela and Jess—not again today.

"Hurry, Miss J!" I said. "I think we can lose them."

"Wait!" Angela called. "I've been looking everywhere for you."

Miss Jackson stopped pushing me then. "You have?" I stiffened a little, you know, waiting for some mean joke, starring me as the punch line.

"Sure," Angela said. "Did you forget we're partners in math class? You want to win Mr. Postin's scavenger hunt, don't you?"

I blinked. Was she serious? Forget about figuring out middle school. I wasn't sure I'd even figure out Angela.

Then it happened. Angela smiled, a for-real smile. I even looked around, just to be sure she was really smiling at me and not some kid standing behind me. I hate when that happens.

"Uh-huh, yeah," I finally said. Wait a minute. The most popular girl in school is actually speaking to me, and I sound like a giant dork. "I mean, of course I want to win the scavenger hunt."

Angela's smile got even bigger. "So let's talk about it on the way to lunch." She looked at Miss Jackson. "Do you mind if I push Mia to the cafeteria?"

Miss J looked at me. "It's up to you."

"Sure," I said. "That would be awesome. Thank you, Angela."

"You're welcome," Angela said.

We were off to the lunch room again. Angela pushed me, with Jess and Miss J right behind. Usually, it bugged me when people stared at me but not today. I even sat up a little straighter in my chair, hoping everyone would notice that I, Mia Lee, was hanging out with her, Miss Popular Angela Vanover.

"So are you busy after school today, Mia?" Angela asked as we got closer to the cafeteria. "I was thinking we could hang out after math class to find all the numbers for the scavenger hunt. My mom can drive us around town to get some pictures and then drive you home afterward, too, if that works for you."

"That sounds good," I said. That totally worked for me. For once, I was hanging out with a popular girl instead of doodling a Middle School Monster cartoon. I already imagined Angela laughing at some hilarious joke I just told while we snapped pictures for the scavenger hunt. Hey, this could be my big chance. Maybe I could even get into Angela's group of friends. As soon as those words came out of my mouth, I wasn't so sure it would work for one person—Mom.

See, Mom had this thing about getting to know the parents of people I was friends with before she'd let me go places with them. She was afraid somebody would try to kidnap me or something. No matter how many times I told her people were into stealing bikes, not wheelchairs, she still insisted on meeting other kids' parents.

But how could I tell Angela that? She'd think I was lame, for sure.

"Wow!" Angela said. "You must have a cool mom. Mine never lets me hang out with anyone until she meets them first and their parents," she added, rolling her eyes and laughing.

It was like Angela had read my mind. *Come clean, Mia,* I told myself. *Angela will get it since her mom is overprotective, too.*

But then Angela went on about the places we'd go after school, and how awesome it would be to win the scavenger hunt. So even though I wanted to tell her the truth—that I'd have to check with my mom first—I couldn't.

Angela ended with, "So we're all set. See ya in math class!" Then she disappeared into the long line of hungry T-W middle schoolers. Miss Jackson was there to help me get my lunch.

"Which line would you like, Mia?"

There were two lines. One was for the daily meal. Today, that was chicken nuggets, fries, and fruit cups. The other was "à la carte." That meant we got to choose what we wanted. Mom and Ella would probably want me to grab something there, too, like salad or celery sticks. But it was only the second day of school, so I stuck with the nuggets. They seemed safe enough. I'd heard stories about middle school meals: mystery meats and hot dogs that bounced and year-old baked beans. No thanks.

"Where's Caroline?" Miss Jackson asked. She knew we always ate lunch together.

I scanned the crowd until I finally spotted a jacket with a fuzzy horse on the back. It was all 3-D, with hair for a mane and everything. Anyway, that would be Caroline.

"Over there." I pointed to the corner table where Caroline sat alone at one end, even though there were a few girls on the other end.

"There you are!" Caroline said when she saw me. "I saved you a seat."

"Thanks," I said. Miss Jackson put my tray on the table and helped me get settled across from Caroline before she headed off to grab her own lunch.

"So how's day two at T-W Middle?" I asked, sipping my juice box.

I waited for Caroline to swallow the chicken salad wrap she was chewing. That was her usual lunch for as long as I could remember. That was also another Caroline quirk. She never liked to mix things up—not her meals, not the books she read, and not even where she shopped. Like if I asked Caroline right now where she bought the horse earrings she wore, she'd say Forever Style, her forever favorite store. But hey, it made being her best friend easy. Birthday? No stress because Caroline always loved the Forever Style gift cards I gave her.

Caroline wiped her mouth and said, "Not bad except my locker hates me. I'm convinced that the combination changes every time I try to put my stuff away."

"I'm pretty sure your locker doesn't hate you. It just has to get to know you," I joked.

"Nope, it hates me, for sure," Caroline said. "It took me three tries to get it open before lunch. Three!"

"I'm sorry," I said. I really did feel bad for Caroline because, thanks to Miss Jackson, I had zero locker problems.

"And," she went on, "I didn't have a partner in science class because you weren't in there with me."

Caroline hated change when it came to making new friends, too. Now that we didn't have many classes together, I couldn't be her partner all the time. And in math class, Mr. Postin had assigned us different partners. So I hoped Caroline would give some other kids a chance.

"Guess what?" I changed the subject.

"I know what," Caroline said. "I saw Angela pushing you into the cafeteria. What's up with that?"

I shrugged. "Nothing. Angela just wants to work on our scavenger hunt project for Mr. Postin's class. She wants to be friends, I guess."

Caroline made a face, like she didn't believe it. "Angela? *Your* friend? I doubt it."

Okay, so that stung a little. Why *wouldn't* Angela want to be friends with me? Caroline, of all people, should know what a great friend I was. But I wasn't so great at keeping a straight face or hiding how I feel. Like, I always stunk at playing Truth or Dare because my lips always twisted a little to one side when I didn't exactly tell the truth.

Anyway, Caroline must've noticed what she'd said about Angela not being my friend had hurt my feelings because she said, "No, I'm sorry. I totally didn't mean it like that, Mia. It's just, yesterday Angela was really mean to you. And today, she's suddenly nice." Caroline shook her head. "Something's up with her."

"Maybe we were wrong about Angela being a mean girl yesterday," I said. "Everybody can have a bad day, especially on the first day at a new school, right?"

"I guess so," Caroline said. But she still didn't look like she believed that was why Angela was being nice to me now.

"Guess what?" I said again, hoping to drop this subject, too.

"What?" Caroline asked.

"Ms. Randells yelled at me in English class."

"No way!" I thought Caroline was going to choke on her wrap. "But all of the Bellmont teachers loved you."

"Yep, but this isn't Bellmont," I reminded her.

Just then, Rory and Daniela walked by with their trays. At first, they didn't see me, so I waved. "Rory! Daniela! Come sit with us!" I called. When they saw me, they both smiled.

Caroline didn't smile, though; instead, she frowned. "I was hoping it would just be us," she said real low.

"You'll like these girls. They're super cool, I promise."

Caroline still didn't look too convinced, but Rory and Daniela bounced over then. "Hey, Mia!"

I grinned. "Hey, guys! This is Caroline. Caroline, you know Rory from Bellmont, right? And this is Daniela," I said, pointing to everyone as I introduced them. "Rory and Daniela are in my English class."

They both waved at Caroline. Rory said, "Hey, Caroline!"

"Hi," Caroline said back. Instead of looking at Rory, Caroline stared at the lettuce poking from her half-eaten chicken wrap, like it was going to talk to her.

"So can you believe we have English homework already?" I asked, hoping Caroline would warm up a little. "We've gotta write about ourselves."

Caroline brightened up a notch. "I know. I had English earlier, too. I love writing."

That reminded me I still hadn't told her about my latest Mean Middle School Monster cartoon idea, starring Angela. Now that Angela was being nice to me, it looked like we'd probably have to look for a new Mean Middle School Monster star. But I didn't want to talk about it in front of Rory and Daniela because I didn't know them that well yet.

Daniela nodded. "I've been thinking all day about what to write about. Maybe it'll be about my family. I have four brothers and sisters."

"Wow!" I said. "That's a lot. I only have one sister, Ella. She's away at college."

"Do you miss her?" Daniela asked.

"Sometimes," I said. "But I like hanging out just me and my mom, too."

"Oh, did your parents split?" Daniela asked, drizzling honey mustard sauce on her nuggets.

I shook my head. "No. My dad teaches college kids in Beijing about history and stuff. He'll be here over winter break, though."

"Cool! My grandparents live in Mexico. I get to see them over winter break, too," Daniela said. Then she squeezed a whole packet of sauce right onto her tongue.

"So I'm guessing you really, really like honey mustard, huh, Daniela?" Rory said, laughing.

Daniela licked her lips. "How could you tell?" She laughed, too.

Meeting new people at T-W Middle was fun. Plus, seeing everyone else's quirks, like Daniela squeezing honey mustard right into her mouth, helped me not freak out so much about this writing assignment.

Except, apparently, I was still freaking out about it. I turned toward Rory then. "So what are you going to write about?" I half hoped she was in the same boat as me, the USS Writer's Block.

"I'm going to write about Roofus," she said.

"What's a Roofus?" Daniela asked.

Rory smiled. "Roofus isn't a what. It's a who. Roofus is my Labrador retriever. He's a-stinking-dorable!"

"Labrador retrievers are cool dogs," Caroline said.

"You'll have to meet Roofus some time," Rory said, "all of you."

Caroline was finally coming around. Besides horses, she also really liked dogs. That's because she couldn't have one of those in her apartment either. I was happy Caroline was giving Rory and Daniela a chance.

"I couldn't believe Ms. Randells was mad at you after you helped her find her earring," Daniela said to me.

"Me neither!" I responded. It wasn't like I usually did anything to even make any teachers mad at me.

Daniela joked, "I thought she was going to erupt."

We all laughed when Daniela made spewing volcano sounds.

Then Rory said, "I still can't believe you figured out Ms. Randells's earring was in her scarf so fast."

I shrugged. "I guess my brain is sort of like the wall of post-it notes behind Mrs. Wheatley's desk in the library."

"Post-it notes?" Rory asked.

"Yeah. Mrs. Wheatley practically wallpapered one entire wall with post-its," I said. "You guys didn't see it?"

Rory, Daniela, and Caroline all shook their heads.

"Anyway, when I'm in my wheelchair, I have tons of time to notice stuff that most other people don't. So I sort of jot down notes about people and lots of different stuff and store it all right here." I smiled and tapped my head.

"So let me get this straight, it's like your brain is covered in post-it notes," Rory said.

"Sort of." I smiled. "Except I call them my Brain Files. I update them every time I learn something new that I want to remember."

"Trust me, Mia has tons of files," Caroline chimed in.

"That's so cool!" Daniela said. "It was also cool the way you stood up for me to those boys in English class."

"You what?" Caroline looked surprised.

Daniela smiled. "You should've seen her in action." Then she told Caroline the whole story about the boys picking on her, and how I'd come to her "rescue." That part was a little embarrassing.

"Wow!" Caroline looked at me. "That's awesome!"

"Thanks," I said. "But it wasn't that big of a deal."

Daniela shook her head. "Don't listen to her. It totally was a huge deal."

"Hey! I just got an idea," Caroline said. "Maybe you should use that for your Video Production Club campaign."

My campaign! I really hadn't given it too much thought yet. But I didn't get how what happened in English class had anything to do with my VP Club campaign.

"Yeah," Caroline went on. "We can make posters with your face and like a superhero's body. Trust me, it'll look amazing."

I scrunched up my nose. "I'm not so sure about that."

"I didn't know you were running for VP Club president," Rory said. "But Caroline's right. Everybody loves superheroes."

"No doubt," Daniela agreed.

"Okay, I'll think about the superhero posters," I promised, adding, "So I even have to make this campaign video to earn points for the election." I tugged the VP Club rules sheet from my backpack and plopped it on the table for everyone to read. There were tons of instructions, like that videos were limited to five minutes. They had to be burned onto a DVD for judging, and they must be the original work of the students.

Caroline, Rory, and Daniela skimmed through the rules.

Rory pointed to number three: *Other students are permitted to assist VP Club presidential candidates with campaign videos.*

"So we'll all help you with your video, Mia," Rory said.

Caroline and Daniela nodded in agreement.

"Great!" I said. "But there's only one teeny problem."

"What?" Caroline asked.

"How do I earn points?" I pointed at the rules sheet. "I mean, this doesn't even say how the campaign videos are scored."

"Oh, gotcha," Daniela said. "It's like you don't know what to focus on to make your video supergreat if you don't know how points are awarded."

"Exactly," I said. "I even asked Mr. Postin about scoring some points. He just said not to get hung up on earning points, that all students should just do their best work."

Rory frowned. "So why is this some big secret?"

Yeah, it was sort of like this whole thing had "*Top Secret*" stamped across it. Mr. Postin definitely wanted to keep it that way. But then I thought about the last script Ella had written for my stop-motion video. Saige had a friend with a major secret, and Saige snooped through her friend's bedroom until she found out what the secret was. Snooping around in someone else's stuff wasn't cool—ever. But Saige did it to help her friend. So in the end, she did it for the right reason. Plus, it all made for a juicy video.

Anyway, it wasn't too late to find out how to score VP Club campaign video points. Maybe I could still find out on my own, sort of like Saige did in the video. "Thanks, Rory."

"You're welcome, but what did I do?" she asked.

"See, you just reminded me of a stop-motion video I made."

"Stop-motion—what's that?" Rory said.

"Stop-motion videos are where you take lots of pictures of something, like a doll. When you put them all together, it makes the doll look like it's moving," I explained.

"I get it." Daniela said. "I've seen cartoons like that."

"Exactly." I said. "Stop-motion videos are used a lot in animation." Then I told them all about the video with Saige.

Rory's eyes widened. "You mean, you want to snoop around in Mr. Postin's classroom?"

"Geez, Louise." I laughed. "No, I meant Saige didn't stop until she got some answers. So why should I?"

"Are you serious?" Caroline asked.

I nodded. "As can be. Except, instead of snooping around, I'll figure out when nobody else is in Mr. Lewis M. Postin's classroom. Then we can stop by to talk about my VP Club campaign when he's alone. And maybe Mr. Postin will just, you know, happen to spill it about scoring VP points." I smiled. "I mean, teachers get sidetracked all the time, right?"

"Wait a minute. How do you know Mr. Postin's middle initial?" Rory asked.

I shrugged. "It was in the T-W Middle faculty guide they handed out to us at our very first assembly."

"I didn't know anybody actually read that stuff," Rory said. "I'm starting to think nothing gets by you, Mia."

I smiled again. Rory was right. Not a lot got past me. I guess paying attention to details was one perk of being in a wheelchair. And paying close attention usually helped me do really well on tests and stuff. So why not use it this time to help me win this election, too?

"Uh-oh. Check it out, Mia," Daniela said. "You're not the only one serious about winning this election. I think Angela is pretty serious, too."

That's when I saw it: Angela's campaign poster. She'd just taped a picture of herself up on the cafeteria wall. Angela looked movie star perfect—no surprise. Above her perfect head, in perfect letters, it read: *Vote Angela Vanover for VP Club President.* And as if she really was some movie star autographing a poster, *Angela Vanover* was scrawled across the bottom in her perfectly looped cursive handwriting. So Angela's campaign poster was pretty much just like the way she looked—perfect.

"Angela went to my old elementary school," Daniela said. "Miss Popular doesn't like to lose—ever."

Okay, so there *was* one little thing that I'd forgotten all about—Angela. She was my VP Club president opponent. Yesterday, I wanted to beat her to win this election. But now that Angela was talking to me, I had my chance to fit in with her and with the group of popular kids that she was the leader of.

How could I run for VP Club president *and* be friends with Angela? Did I even want to run against her now? I wasn't sure. Middle school was now more confusing than ever.

Chapter Six: What An Angel

After math class that afternoon, Caroline said, "Hey, Mia! Do you want to come over to my house to hang out for a few hours? It's your turn to pick what movie we watch."

"She can't!" Angela came over and answered for me. "We're busy looking for all of the numbers on our scavenger hunt list so we can win. See ya."

It was sort of like Angela dismissed Caroline. I could tell Caroline expected me to say something, but I couldn't, you know. I mean, didn't Caroline get it? I was just getting in good with Angela now. When I got in really good with Angela and with all of her friends, then I'd try to get Caroline into the group, too. But for now, I had to hang out with Angela by myself without Caroline.

"I'm sorry," I said to Caroline. "But we did already have plans. Maybe next time."

"Okay," Caroline said.

I still felt bad for Caroline, but I couldn't think about her any more right now because Angela grabbed my wheelchair handles and took off pushing me down the hallway. "My mom is running late, but she'll be here to pick us up soon," Angela said.

I'd texted Mom and begged her to let me leave T-W Middle to work on the scavenger hunt with Angela. I even told her Angela's mom would drive me home when we were finished with our project. Mom texted back one word: *No!*

Now I had to quickly come up with some excuse about why I couldn't leave the school to work on the scavenger hunt with Angela. It had to be something good, too.

"Yeah, about that. See, I get really carsick, and I haven't taken my medicine for motion sickness today. I don't want to, you know, puke all in your mom's car or anything."

That sort of wasn't an excuse, though, because it was the truth. I really did get carsick a lot. The last time it happened was back in the summer when Mom, Dad, Ella, and I had taken a road trip to see the Grand Canyon. Usually, I was fine for short distances, but it was probably better not to risk it.

Angela looked sort of grossed out at first, but then she said, "No problem. We can work on our project in the library, I guess. I'll just let Mom know to pick me up a little later." She whipped out her phone to text her mom. Then she slid it back into her pocket and took off pushing me down the hallway again.

"Wait! This is the wrong way. The library is that way," I said, pointing. "Remember?"

Angela sort of did this fake laugh. "I know, but I see some kids from the Video Production Club over there. Let's go say hi."

When Angela pushed me over to them, she said, "Hey, guys!" Then she made a big show of locking my wheelchair brakes. "We don't want you rolling off, Mia." Angela even patted my shoulder.

Some of the VP Club kids smiled. It made me feel weird, though, like I was all of a sudden Angela's community service project or something. But all of the kids from VP Club looked as if the T-W Middle School ceiling had just opened up and a holy light from heaven shone down on Angela Vanover, the middle school saint. Seriously, she could drop the *a* on the end of her name, and everyone could all call her Angel from now on.

Angela leaned over my wheelchair to get closer. Then she said real loud in my ear, "Are you ready to go to the library, Mia?"

I'd never hung out with popular kids before. So I wondered if being superpopular meant Angela talked real loud to all of her friends. Did her friends answer her back real loud, too? I decided they probably did. So I practically shouted back, "Ready, Angela!"

So she unlocked my wheelchair brakes, and we were off to the library. When we were out of sight of the VP Club kids, Angela stopped. "You can push yourself in this thing, right?"

"Sure," I said. Then I put my hands on the wheels and wheeled myself a few feet to show her.

"Good." Angela said. "But if we're going to find everything on our list before everyone else does, you're gonna have to push yourself faster than that. Hurry up!"

Angela took off down the hallway, but there was no way I could wheel myself that fast. By the time I caught up with Angela again, she was near Mr. Postin's classroom.

When I was just outside Mr. Postin's door, Angela suddenly came running toward me. Then she started talking real loud again. "Mia, let me push you." She grabbed my wheelchair handles, taking over to push me.

"But I thought you wanted me to push myself," I said.

"No, don't be silly," Angela said, still louder than normal. "I'm happy to help you."

Angela kept confusing me. I couldn't figure her out, so I decided it was time to log another Brain File on her.

Subject: Angela (again!)

Weird Factor: First, she wanted to push my wheelchair. Then two minutes ago, she wanted me to push myself. Now she wants to push me again.

Even Weirder: Angela talks really loud, but only sometimes, like just now when the VP Club kids and Mr. Postin were around.

Still Unknown: What gives with this girl?

By now, Mr. Postin was looking at us from his desk. "Hello, girls. Working hard on your scavenger hunt project I take it?"

"Yes, sir," Angela said.

"That's what I like to hear." Mr. Postin smiled. "Good luck."

"Thanks," Angela and I both said at the same time.

Angela took off pushing me again, this time inside the library.

"Isn't Mrs. Wheatley one of the judges who'll choose the VP Club video winner?" Angela asked.

"I think so," I said.

"Perfect!" So Angela paraded me past Mrs. Wheatley's desk before finally pushing me over to an empty corner table.

"Now," she said, plopping down on a chair and pulling our scavenger hunt list from her backpack, "let's see what we can find on here."

"Maybe we should divide the list," I suggested.

"Good idea." Angela started to rip the sheet of paper in half.

"No!" I stopped her. "I meant divide it up. Like you choose some things to find, and I'll choose some other things."

"That's even better," Angela agreed. Then she got out a clean sheet of paper and started jotting down a few things she planned to find.

This was the closest I'd ever been to Angela, at least, when she wasn't cracking some mean joke about me. So while she worked on the list, I checked out Angela's makeup. It was flawless. I wondered what the shimmery pastel purple eye shadow that highlighted Angela's blue eyes would look like with my brown eyes. I wasn't even allowed to wear lip gloss yet. I always thought other girls whose moms let them wear makeup were superlucky.

Angela looked up and caught me staring at her. I didn't want to look like a creeper, so I said, "Your makeup is supercool. My mom has this dumb no-makeup-until-I'm-thirteen rule."

Angela laughed. "I've been wearing makeup since I was like two years old."

"No way!" I almost didn't believe her. "When I was two, I'm pretty sure I would've used a tube of lipstick to draw on the walls, not to wear on my lips," I joked.

"It's not like I put it on myself back then. My mom put it on me for beauty pageants. She says you're never too young to enhance your natural beauty."

That was kind of weird. But I could picture baby Angela, with her perfect hair and makeup, toddling around in a tiara.

"Are you still into pageants?" I asked.

"Of course," Angela said, still writing. "I have this big state competition next month. Mom's really excited about that one."

I noticed something then. Besides details, I'm also really good at reading people, like their expressions and how they feel and stuff. Angela didn't seem too excited about this pageant. Now that we were becoming friends, I decided to ask her, "So what about you?"

"What about me?" Angela looked up from the list.

"Are you excited about the pageant, too?"

She sort of smiled when she said, "Pageants are what I do. And Mom has big plans for me to compete in the Miss USA pageant someday."

Even though Angela's face had a smile pasted on it, her eyes weren't smiling. Pageants may be what she did, but I wasn't so sure she was as happy about competing in them—at least, not as much as her mom was.

Angela shrugged and said, "Okay, back to this scavenger hunt. I've jotted down some things I'll find." She handed me the list. "And I've circled some things for you to find. Go!"

We took off in different directions. I had to find a fraction. First, I wheeled myself around the library, looking at the posters on the wall for a fraction. Nothing.

"Can I help you with something, Mia?" Mrs. Wheatley asked.

"Not unless you're hiding a fraction somewhere," I said.

Mrs. Wheatley looked puzzled.

So I told her about the scavenger hunt and how I had to find a fraction to take a picture of.

"Think about all of the places you might use a fraction, perhaps even in the kitchen," Mrs. Wheatley said with a wink.

"I got it! A recipe," I said. "Thanks, Mrs. Wheatley."

I wheeled myself over to the shelves until I found a whole section of recipe books. I grabbed one and flipped to a lasagna recipe: one-fourth teaspoon of oregano. Perfect.

But I couldn't hold the book *and* snap a picture at the same time. It took both of my hands to hold my phone steady. I tried setting the book on the shelf, with the page open to the recipe. That didn't work either. The book kept toppling over. So then I got the idea to put the book on the floor and hold it open to the right page with the toe of my sneaker. Then I could snap the picture. It worked.

"That's one way to do it, I guess." Angela was coming down the same aisle.

"Yeah," I said. "I'm used to figuring out different ways to do stuff. So if you're ever cooking and need someone to hold a recipe with their feet, call me."

Angela flashed me a weird look and said, "Will do."

Why did I say the dumbest things when Angela was around? Also, why did I have to draw attention to my plain, boring sneakers in front of Angela when she wore the cutest boots ever? I really wished I could wear boots, too. But because they wouldn't fit around my braces, I was stuck wearing clunky sneakers.

"So how many things have you found?" Angela asked.

"Counting this fraction?" I pretended to count. "Um, that makes...one."

"Seriously?" Angela asked. "You're going to have to work faster, or we'll never get pictures of everything on our scavenger hunt list today."

"I'm sorry," I said.

Then Angela talked to me in this superslow voice, like I had a problem understanding stuff. "Listen. If we lose, it'll be all your fault, Mia."

I really didn't like it when people slowed down their words when they talked to me. My problem was with my legs and with my hands, not my brain. I couldn't tell Angela that I didn't like the way she talked to me, though—not yet. Our friendship was still too new, and I didn't want to make her mad. Then Angela might kick me out of her group before I even really got in it.

"I'm sorry," I said again. Really, I wasn't sure what I was sorry for. For being slower than Angela because I'm in a wheelchair? For it being my fault if we lost the scavenger hunt project? Or was I sorry that I minded the way Angela talked to me just then? Angela just had this way of making me feel sorry about lots of stuff, I guess.

"Stop saying you're sorry and work on the project already!" Angela snapped.

Geez, Louise! Being friends with Angela was hard. Being friends with Caroline seemed easier somehow. But my physical therapist told me once when we were doing some really tough exercises that anything worth having meant hard work. I figured that was true with Angela's friendship, too.

So I started talking about our scavenger hunt list again. "Next on my list is a date in time," I said. "That shouldn't be hard to find in a history book or maybe even a newspaper."

"I have to find a degree," Angela said. "I picked that because I thought it would be easy to find a temperature, but there's no thermometer in here."

So Angela purposefully picked things for herself that she thought would be easier to find, huh? I guess I sort of couldn't blame her.

Then I thought of something. "The list just said a degree, right?"

Angela checked the list again. "Right."

"So it doesn't *have* to be a temperature."

Now Angela looked at me like I was really losing it. "If it's not a temperature, what other degree could there be?"

"Think about it," I said. "A map has degrees, too. There are degrees of latitude and longitude. And"—I pointed to the wall—"there's a world map right over there."

"Perfect! Why don't you try working as hard as me, Mia?" Angela said before taking off to snap a picture.

Was she kidding? Unbelievable! I shook my head and mumbled "You're welcome" to myself. Then I headed over to ask Mrs. Wheatley for a newspaper. Before I wheeled myself over there, Angela was already back.

"Look! My mom's here," she said.

I looked in the direction where Angela pointed. *That* was her mom? The lady walking toward us didn't look like any mom I'd ever seen. I mean, my mom practically lived in sweats but not Angela's mom. In her tailored jacket, tight-fitting skirt, and strappy high heels, she looked like she hopped off the cover of some fashion magazine. She was just like Angela—perfect.

"Good news, Angela," her mom said. "I already have all the pictures you need for your math scavenger hunt right here." She waved her phone around.

"Really? Thanks, Mom!" Angela hugged her.

"You're welcome," Angela's mom said, smoothing the front of her jacket as if Angela's hug had wrinkled it. "You can just download the pictures from my phone to yours. And voilà! Your math project is history." She laughed at her own joke.

Hopefully, this whole thing was a joke. In case it wasn't, I piped up with, "Hang on. Mr. Postin said we have to work together and take the pictures ourselves."

"Forget Mr. Postin," Angela said. "If we don't tell him, he'll never know we didn't take the pictures ourselves. And *I'm* not telling him. Are you?"

I got out of sneaking off with Angela today and then lying to Mom about it. But now Angela wanted me to say we'd taken some pictures for our project that we really didn't. I'd be lying to Mr. Postin, my favorite teacher so far. That definitely wasn't how I wanted to kick off my middle school year.

"I don't know," I finally said.

"Look, everybody needs help sometimes," Angela's mom began. Instead of looking at me when she said it, she checked out my wheelchair. That's the way it always was when I met somebody new for the first time: they saw my wheelchair first. Then they noticed me second. Her gaze shifted from the footrests that supported my legs up to my eyes. "So that's all I'm doing here, helping you girls out a little."

A little? She'd finished our entire project for us.

"Angela needs to focus on her VP Club campaign," her mom went on. "Lots of big stars get discovered through their online videos, and this could be Angela's big break. Angela doesn't want to blow this. And"—she looked at Angela—"I made you an appointment with Felipe at the salon this afternoon to get your hair and makeup done so you can begin filming your VP Club video."

I looked at Angela, too, but she didn't say anything. I wondered if Angela was worried about blowing the VP Club campaign or if her mom was the one who was worried—sort of like when Angela was talking about beauty pageants earlier. I decided to log a quick Brain File on Angela's mom, too.

Subject: Angela's mom

Alias: Mrs. Vanover

Note: Seems more like some manager wannabe than a mom.

Still Unknown: Possible control freak?

Angela's mom tapped her watch. "We can't be late for your appointment, so tell your friend good-bye."

Hey, Angela's mom called me Angela's friend! That must've meant Angela had at least talked about me to her mom at home before now, right?

"Later, Mia," Angela said, adding, "Trust me, this scavenger hunt thing is no biggie."

I squirmed in my chair. Lying to Mr. Postin about our project felt like a biggie to me. But if I really was Angela's friend, like her mom had said, I really did have to trust her, didn't I?

Chapter Seven: Phone Swap Gone Sour

Before homeroom the next morning, I hung out around my locker with Caroline, Rory, and Daniela.

"So did you have fun with Angela yesterday?" Caroline asked.

"*You* hung out with Miss Perfect?" Daniela asked.

"What's she like?" Rory chimed in.

I held up my hands. "Geez, Louise! Slow down with the questions, guys." But then I answered each question, starting with Caroline's. "We just worked on our scavenger hunt project, you know, so I wouldn't exactly call it fun." Next was Daniela's question. "Yes, we did hang out at the library." And then there was Rory's. "Angela is, well, let's just say I've never met anyone like her."

That was true, and it seemed like a good way to put it. I'd never met anyone so hard to figure out. One minute, I felt like her new best friend, but the next, not so much.

"Enough about Angela," I said. "So remember the other day when I said I'd find out when Mr. Postin was in his classroom alone so we could get in there to talk to him about how to score points for my Video Production Club campaign?"

Rory and Daniela nodded. Caroline said, "You're still planning on doing that, Mia?"

"Yep, and I've almost got it figured out. So—"

"Mia! Over here!" It was Angela. She motioned me toward her.

"Sorry," I said to Caroline, Rory, and Daniela. "I'll fill you in later. I promise."

Then I wheeled myself over to where Angela stood near her locker.

She leaned down and whispered, "I have all of the pictures we need for our scavenger hunt downloaded onto my phone. I'll turn them into Mr. Postin right now, so we'll win. If he asks any questions, let me handle it." She stood back up. "Got it?"

"Got it," I said. I still didn't want to go through with Angela's idea to turn in work that we didn't do, though. Her mom had taken almost all of our pictures for us.

"Good." Angela started to walk away.

"Wait," I said. "Do you want to come over to my house today? My mom really wants to meet you."

"Um." Angela seemed to think about it before saying "no."

"Oh," I said. Okay, I really didn't expect that. Maybe Angela was just shy meeting new people. I guessed I was being a little too pushy too soon. "I'm sorry," I added. Here I went, apologizing to Angela again.

She waved her hand, dismissing me, sort of like how she'd dismissed Caroline yesterday.

My mouth sort of dropped open, I think. Then someone rushed toward me. I'm not sure who was there first—Caroline, Rory, or Daniela. It was hard to see through the blurry tears stinging my eyes.

The rest of the day passed in a blur, too, until lunch. Caroline, Rory, Daniela, and I grabbed a table. It was sort of becoming *our* table already.

"I forgot napkins," Caroline said. "I'll be right back."

While she was gone, I reached for her phone. Caroline and I swapped phones all the time. That's because when you've been friends as long as we have, you don't mind sharing your text messages or videos you've made with each other.

I'd just finished watching the video Caroline had made of herself bopping around with sunglasses on the back of her head. "She looks like some crazy rocker dude," I said. Rory, Daniela, and I laughed our heads off.

But the next video wasn't so funny.

"Who is that?" Rory asked, coming in for a closer look.

"It's Angela," I said. "But why does Caroline have a video of Angela on her phone?"

"I can't hear it," Daniela said. "Turn it up some."

I did. Angela was talking to someone—Jess maybe? "Yeah, she's such a weirdo. I don't really like her. But if I want to win the VP Club election, I have to be nice to her to get more votes." She laughed. "And I'm making sure the people voting see me being nice to her."

"Good idea!" Yep, even though she wasn't actually seen in the video, that was definitely Jess's voice.

Then it was like Angela looked up, and Caroline stopped recording real quick.

"What are you doing?" Caroline plopped back down across from me with a stack of napkins.

I held up her phone. "Watching this video of Angela."

"Give me it!" Caroline snatched her phone back. "You weren't supposed to see that."

"What's the big deal? We always swap phones," I said.

Caroline didn't say anything.

"So?" I looked at Caroline.

"So what?" Caroline said, but she wouldn't look at me.

"So who is the weirdo that Angela was talking about in that video?" I asked.

Caroline still didn't say anything.

"C'mon, Caroline. Tell us." I laughed. "Whoever it is sounds like a real nerd."

Rory and Daniela sort of laughed, too.

"Stop it!" Caroline slammed her juice box down on the table. Good thing she had all of those napkins. She needed them to clean that mess up. But she wasn't too worried about spilled juice right now. "It's you, okay?" Caroline said. "Angela was talking about you in that video, Mia."

Now it was my turn not to say anything. I mean, what did I say to that? Then I got it. I knew exactly what was going on here. "Caroline, you're the one who needs to stop. You're just saying that stuff because I'm in Angela's group and you're not."

"Hello!" Caroline said. "Did you already forget the way Angela treated you this morning?"

Of course I remembered the way Angela had acted all mean again this morning. But I didn't hold it against her or anything. It wasn't like she could be in a good mood all the time. Who could? I'd probably just upset Angela when I'd asked her to come to my house to meet my mom when she wasn't ready yet. That was my fault.

Caroline was making up that Angela was talking about me in that video, and I decided to call her out on it. "So if she was talking about me, how come I didn't hear my name on the video? Angela just said 'she' and 'her,' but she never said my name." I took a deep breath. "So explain that one."

"That's because Jess asked Angela, 'So do you really like Mia?' When I heard your name, that's when I started recording. They didn't say your name again after that," Caroline said.

I guess she could tell I still didn't buy it.

"I recorded the video because I knew you wouldn't believe it if I told you," Caroline explained. "And even though you saw the video for yourself, you still don't believe it."

"You just don't know Angela like I do," I said. "I was going to try to get you in her group, too, once I got in good with her. But now"—I shook my head—"I may not."

"Fine!" Caroline said. "I don't want to be in Angela's dumb group anyway. And I'm not so sure I want to be in yours anymore either!" Then Caroline grabbed what was left of her chicken wrap and stormed off.

"Double fine!" I called after Caroline. I doubt she heard me because the bell rang just then.

Chapter Eight: Coming Clean

"We have our scavenger hunt winners!" Mr. Postin announced in math class that afternoon. "Angela Vanover and Mia Lee, would you two ladies please come forward?"

Angela was the first one up front. By holding on to each desk in front of mine, I slowly made my way to the front of the room, too. When I turned around to face the class, Mr. Postin said, "Let's give Mia and Angela a round of applause for their hard work!"

The entire class clapped—well, except one person. Caroline didn't clap. She didn't look too happy for me either. Her face was all scrunched up and red. She looked like a mad tomato.

What Caroline didn't know, though, was that I wasn't even happy for myself. How could I be when the photographs Mr. Postin saw weren't taken by me or my scavenger hunt partner, Angela? They were actually taken by Angela's mom.

"Please tell us," Mr. Postin went on, "how did you girls finish your assignment so quickly? Some of the numbers must have been hard to find."

"Well, honestly..." I began, but then Angela nudged me, and I remembered what she said earlier about letting her handle it if Mr. Postin asked any questions about our project. So I closed my mouth real quick.

"I think what Mia started to say is that, honestly, we worked together really well. And that's how we got it finished super fast," Angela said, smiling.

I couldn't take the extra attention anymore. I grabbed the desk next to me and started making my way back toward my seat again. But Mr. Postin wasn't finished talking about the scavenger hunt yet.

"Before we begin dividing decimals today, I'd like for us all to take a look at Mia and Angela's winning photos," Mr. Postin said. "I've compiled them into a slideshow."

Just great.

The slideshow started off okay. There was a shot of the world map hanging in the library. Angela had zoomed in on the sixteen degrees above the longitude line slicing through Sweden. I had begged Angela to include my fraction picture instead of her mom's, and she finally agreed. I could even prove I was the photographer because the toe of my sneaker was still in the picture where I had used my foot to hold the recipe book on the right page while I snapped the shot.

As soon as the third picture flashed on the screen, though, I knew there was a real problem with that one. Would anyone else notice? See, one of the things on our list was to find a ninety-degree right angle. Angela's mom had found one all right. She'd taken a picture of a statue that's situated in a park downtown. In the background was a clock, with a time of 1:15 p.m. We were still in school then, so there's no way we could've taken that picture. What was Angela's mom thinking? How could Angela *not* have noticed that when she'd downloaded the pictures to her phone?

By the time the next picture popped up, no one had said a word. At the end of the slideshow, I held my breath. Nope. Still no mention of the time on the clock. We were apparently safe. But being a criminal felt crummy. Angela might not like it, but we had to confess. We had to tell Mr. Postin the truth. We would—after class.

Mr. Postin worked some division problems out on the board. Then he helped some kids who still couldn't solve the problems on their own. While he did that, the rest of us were supposed to start on homework. I couldn't, though. I had to talk to Angela. Now!

When I tapped Angela on her shoulder, she whirled around and snapped, "What now?"

"Nothing. I just…Oh, Angela," I whispered, "I can't do it. I can't lie to Mr. Postin about the scavenger hunt."

"Shh!" She shushed me. Then she glanced around. "Do you want everyone to hear you?"

"No, but I think everyone can figure it out. Didn't you notice the time on the clock in that one picture? There's no way either one of us could have taken that shot."

Angela rolled her eyes. Then she said real slow, "Don't worry about it." She got even slower when she asked, "Un-der-stand?"

"Yeah," I said, glancing over Caroline's way. "I think I'm starting to."

That was the second time Angela had talked to me like I wasn't smart enough to figure things out. And you know, she was right. Because at first, I really couldn't figure out why Angela acted the way she did. But after watching the video on Caroline's phone and the way Angela talked to me just now, I was beginning to figure everything out, even Angela.

I texted Ella real quick.

Mia Lee: How can you tell if someone is a fake?

Ella texted right back.

Ella Lee: Trust your gut. You'll know.

There was that word again—*trust*. Angela had told me to trust her, and I did at first. Now, my gut was screaming at me that Angela Vanover was a fake. Soon, I'd let her know I was on to her.

As soon as class was over and before Angela could leave the classroom, I said, "Mr. Postin, Angela and I need to talk to you."

"Don't," Angela whispered to me.

But it was too late. Mr. Postin shut the door behind the last student to leave. When it was just the three of us in the classroom, he asked, "Is something wrong?"

I nodded. "Yes, sir. It's the scavenger hunt photos."

"Oh?" Mr. Postin folded his arms across his fuzzy sweater vest. "What seems to be the problem?"

"They're not all our pictures," I said.

"Hmm" was all Mr. Postin said.

So I told him which pictures were really ours, like the fraction in the recipe and the degree of longitude on the map. Then I finished with, "But the rest of them were taken by Angela's mom."

"I see." Mr. Postin adjusted his glasses. "What I don't see, though, is why you would use photos that you didn't take on your own."

"It was because of Mia." Angela hadn't said much, but she was making up for it now. "Mia's kind of slow in her wheelchair. So we talked about it and decided we needed some extra help."

"No, we didn't talk about it," I said. "You told me you were using your mom's pictures for our project. It wasn't like I had a choice." We were coming clean with Mr. Postin. No way was I going to let Angela tell another lie.

"Hold on, girls." Mr. Postin held up his hands. "Disregarding the scavenger hunt rules is not acceptable. And whether or not you talked about getting help isn't important right now. What is important is that you realized you made a mistake, and then you decided to tell the truth. That's not always easy to do, and I commend you for that."

"Thank you, Mr. Postin," Angela said, like telling the truth just now was her idea. Mr. Postin turned and headed toward his desk. "Follow me."

When Angela and I were beside Mr. Postin's desk, he said, "You are both disqualified as the scavenger hunt winners. But there must also be consequences for your actions." He handed us a brand-new scavenger hunt list.

"What's this for?" Angela asked.

I thought we were going to get a scavenger hunt do-over, but Mr. Postin had another idea.

"Instead of taking pictures, I want you to write a report on each of the things on this list."

"All of them?" Angela squeaked.

Mr. Postin nodded. "All of them."

Angela groaned, but I knew we'd gotten off lucky, even if it meant writing a report. Geez, Louise! Another report. I still hadn't even started on my English essay yet.

When Angela and I left Mr. Postin's classroom and we were out in the hallway, Angela said, "Thanks a lot, Mia! I hope you're happy."

"I'm not yet," I said. Then I spotted Caroline. "But I'm about to be."

"What's that supposed to mean?" Angela asked.

"You'll find out." Then I waved both hands in the air. "Caroline! Can I talk to you for a sec? Please?"

At first, I didn't think Caroline was going to talk to me. Then she finally came over. "What do you want?"

"I just want to say that I'm sorry for leaving you out the last couple of days. I knew that Angela wasn't very nice to me, unless certain people were around, like Mr. Postin or kids from the VP Club. Then she was supernice, wanting to push my chair and smiling at me and stuff."

"You're crazy!" Angela butted in. "I have no clue what you're even talking about."

"Forget it, Angela," I said. "I saw a video of you saying you were just being nice to me to get more VP Club election votes. And you were making sure everyone saw you being nice to me, too." That's why Angela talked real loud to me when other people were around. She wanted to make sure she got their attention.

"What video?" Angela asked.

"This one." Caroline whipped out her cell phone and played the video for Angela.

As Angela watched, I changed a note in Angela's Brain File.

Still Unknown: What gives with that girl?

Busted: Angela Vanover is a middle school fake!

Angela's face got all red. Then she said, "You're both weirdos."

"Maybe we are, but at least we're not fakes"—I pointed at Angela—"like some people." I went on, "This weirdo girl would never lie to me like you did. She's my best friend. Un-der-stand?" I said it real slow, imitating the way Angela had talked to me earlier.

"Whatever." Angela stomped off.

Caroline and I died laughing.

"Looks like the Middle School Monster, starring Angela Vanover as herself, is back," I said.

"What?" Caroline asked.

"It's a cartoon idea, but"—I waved my hand—"I'll tell you about it later. So are you sure you're not mad at me?"

"I was, but I couldn't stay mad at the coolest girl in school, you big weirdo." Caroline grinned.

I grinned, too. "No, you're the big weirdo."

For the first time in a couple of days, middle school was looking up again—finally! Now that I was definitely on the outside of Angela's group again, I hoped it would last.

Chapter Nine: Points, Points, Points

"I don't know about this, Mia," Caroline whispered, leaning over the back of my wheelchair.

"Just trust me, would you?" I asked.

"Yeah, it's not like we're doing anything wrong," Rory said.

Rory should know, being teacher's pet and everything. "All we have to do is talk to Mr. Postin about the VP Club campaign videos," I said. "Then hopefully, he'll get sidetracked and start talking about how to score points, too."

"Sounds easy," Daniela chimed in.

It took a few days, but by Friday morning, I finally came up with a plan that was guaranteed to let me in on how to score points for my campaign video. Because Angela was my competition, I needed every point I could get. So I told Miss Jackson that I didn't need her help because Caroline, Rory, Daniela, and I had some stuff to work on before school, which was totally true. We really were working on stuff; I just didn't tell Miss J that the stuff we were working on meant heading to Mr. Postin's classroom and getting him to slip up and let us in on scoring points.

See, every day this week, I went by Mr. Postin's classroom at different times to see when he was in there with students and when he was alone. After observing Mr. Postin for a few days, I logged a new Brain File.

Subject: Mr. Postin

Times in Room 117 with Students: First to eighth period, minus sixth period

Times in Room 117 Alone: Before homeroom, 8:30 a.m.–8:50 a.m., a.k.a. right now!

Still Unknown: Top-Secret VP points—how does Mr. Postin award them?

"There he is!" I said. Mr. Postin sat at his desk. No other kids were around. They all hung out around their lockers gabbing. Here was my chance to talk to Mr. Postin with nobody else around.

"Good morning, ladies!" Mr. Postin said when he saw us. "How may I help you?"

"Um," I said.

"Er," Caroline added.

Mr. Postin rested his elbows on the stack of math papers in front of him and smiled. "Well, I'm glad we've got that all cleared up."

Okay, so this wasn't going like I'd planned. Now that I could actually talk to Mr. Postin about scoring VP Club points, I didn't know how to begin.

"It's the VP Club," Daniela jumped in, saving me. "Mia wanted to talk to you about it."

I nodded.

"Yes, the VP Club," Mr. Postin said. "It's such a fun club, and I'm happy you want to be a part of it, Mia. In the fraction picture you took for the math scavenger hunt, I could tell that you have a talented eye for capturing the world in a unique way."

"I do?" I asked. That was a big compliment coming from Mr. Postin. And Mom thought I should be a writer? Wait until I told her what Mr. Postin said about my talented eye.

"Absolutely!" Mr. Postin smiled again. "I just wish there had been more of your pictures included in that assignment."

"Me, too," I said. There would've been if Angela's mom hadn't taken over our project, and if Angela had submitted pictures she and I had taken instead of her mom's. "I'm still sorry about that."

"Principal Williams is dealing with Mrs. Vanover, and I am confident there will never be a problem such as this in the future." Mr. Postin continued, "And speaking of the future, I do look forward to seeing your creativity really shine in your VP Club campaign video."

My campaign video—that was exactly what I'd hoped to talk to Mr. Postin about. I could hardly believe my luck that he brought it up just now. Sweet!

"Yeah, about my video," I said. "I could really use some more information."

"Oh?" Mr. Postin said. "What kind of information do you need, Mia?"

I cleared my throat. "So far, I don't even have any ideas for my video. I was wondering if you could help me come up with something."

"I see," Mr. Postin said. "I'm more than happy to help you, of course."

"Really?" I felt more at ease then. "Thank you, Mr. Postin."

"Sure. The formula for creating your video is quite simple really."

I leaned forward in my wheelchair a little, ready to soak in every word Mr. Postin said, since it would help me to win the VP Club election. Who knew getting information on scoring points for my video would be so easy?

"I encourage you to create a video that covers a topic you're interested in," Mr. Postin went on.

When nobody said anything for a minute, Mr. Postin held up his hands. "There you have it. That's it."

That's it? Mr. Postin tricked me, because how did that help me? Wait, I'll tell you. It didn't.

When I still didn't say anything, Mr. Postin said, "Once you find a topic that interests you, you should have no problem creating a stellar video, Mia. Does that make sense?"

"I guess so," I finally said. "But what about Dalton, last year's VP Club president? What was his video like?"

"Dalton's video was quite impressive," Mr. Postin said. "His video was a documentary that showcased his interest in archaeology. His video went on to be a big hit at our annual VP Club film festival held at the end of the year."

I wrinkled my nose. How could something boring like digging around in the dirt to find old junk win the VP Club presidency? I mean, if that stuff was so great, who would've buried it in the ground in the first place?

Mr. Postin must've read my mind. "It was all in Dalton's presentation. Like I've already said, it goes back to Dalton choosing a topic that mattered to him. You do the same, Mia, and you'll be just fine."

Yeah, right. That was what Mr. Postin thought. He was forgetting one thing: Angela. To win this competition, I had to create the most amazing video the VP Club had ever seen.

"Is there anything else?" Mr. Postin asked.

There definitely was—VP points. Should I just come out and ask Mr. Postin about scoring points for my presentation, or would it be better to just sort of hint around? I wasn't sure.

The first bell rang, warning students to head to homeroom. I was running out of time. "What about earning points for my campaign video?" I blurted out.

Mr. Postin frowned. "I thought we already discussed that."

"Well, sort of," I said. "But you said you don't tell students how the points are awarded."

"Exactly. My lips are sealed," Mr. Postin said.

"It's just, I think it would be helpful to know how points are broken down. Like do we get so many points for creativity, or graphics, or what?" I rushed on.

Mr. Postin made a big deal of zipping his lips. He even pretended to slide a key into his locked lips, turn it, and then toss the invisible key over his shoulder.

"But—" I began.

Mr. Postin tapped his watch and pointed toward the door. I got it! Time for homeroom.

"Thanks, anyway," I said.

Mr. Postin still didn't speak. Instead, he gave me a thumbs-up.

As Caroline pushed me toward the door, Rory said, "Mr. Postin's tough. Let's face it, he's just not giving up any VP points information."

"Yeah," Daniela said. "But at least you tried, Mia."

It looked like I wasn't the only one trying to get more information. When we got closer to the door, someone stood outside, leaning against it. When we got closer, she started to take off, perfect ponytail flying.

"Angela!" I called after her. "Wait!"

She whirled around.

"What were you doing?" I asked.

She smirked. "The question is what were *you* doing, Mia? Trying to get in good with Mr. Postin to score some VP Club points, right?"

"What?" I was surprised.

Angela didn't give me a chance to say anything else because she rushed on with, "But it didn't work because Mr. Postin wouldn't tell you a thing. Besides, don't believe that stuff he said about you having a talented eye." She shook her head. "I bet he only said that because he feels sorry for you." Angela looked pleased with herself.

Geez, Louise! That was supermean, even for Angela, the Meaner-than-Ever Middle School Monster. Regardless, I knew Mr. Postin didn't say I have a talented eye because he felt sorry for me.

I mean, if he felt sorry for me, he would never have called my mom to tell her all about the math scavenger hunt photo fiasco Angela had roped me into. That proved Mr. Postin wasn't into handing out special treatment just because I have a disability. And really, I didn't want any. He treated me just like every other student at T-W Middle. I already liked Mr. Postin, and that made me like him even more.

Angela was bluffing. So I totally ignored what she said. Instead, I asked, "How did you know what Mr. Postin said anyway?" Then I figured it out. "Wait a minute. You were spying on me just now, weren't you?"

Now Angela was the one who looked surprised.

"You were!" I was definitely on to her. "That's why you were standing next to the door. You were eavesdropping."

"Just stuff it!" Angela said, taking off down the hallway.

"Wow! Someone's grouchy this morning," Daniela said, pointing in Angela's direction.

I nodded. "For real. Angela's not even faking it that she's nice to me anymore." I guess I could forget about fitting in with her or her group—ever. But looking up at Caroline, Rory, and Daniela, I decided that was okay. I had my own group. Maybe they weren't the most popular girls in school but so what? They were my *real* friends, not fake friends like Angela.

I was so over Angela, but what I wasn't over was my VP Club campaign video. Even without knowing how to score points, I was going to turn in the best video I could. It would wow Mr. Postin and the judges, just blow 'em away. Too bad there was only one week left to work on it. What was my video even going to be about? I still had to come up with something—soon.

Chapter Ten: Super Mia

"Mom, you've gotta help me come up with some ideas," I said. It was Sunday, and we'd just finished breakfast. I had five days to create my campaign posters *and* my campaign video. Five days!

Mom sipped her coffee. "You wouldn't have this problem if you joined a book club or the school newspaper staff. I'm worried this Video Production Club is too much for you. In fact, when Mr. Postin called to discuss your scavenger hunt assignment, I told him my concerns."

"You didn't!" I said. Just great. Mom probably already ruined my chances of becoming VP Club president. I mean, if Mr. Postin thought I couldn't handle it, I'd never get elected. I'd be lucky to win president of the Losers Club. *Happy now, Mom?*

"I did," Mom said. "Turning in photos that you didn't take for a project just isn't like you, Mia." She shook her head. "I think it's because you're wearing yourself out."

"No way! The whole scavenger hunt thing was all thanks to Angela and her mom, not because I was worn-out," I said. "And no matter what, I don't want to join a reading club. I don't like writing at all!" I reminded Mom for about the ninety-nine millionth time. "I like making videos. Someday, I think I might want to be a movie director even."

"Reading and writing are things you can always do on your own, even when you get older. You already have a hard time making videos. You may not be able to make videos when you get older," Mom said.

"I only have trouble when I use your camera, though."

Mom was right. When I used her big, fancy Canon camera, she always had to help me press the buttons because I couldn't push them on my own. I hardly ever used Mom's camera anyway.

"When I make stop-motions, I usually use my phone and my tripod to keep it steady. That way, I *can* make my videos all by myself, without any help. Besides, you already said I could join the VP Club. Remember?"

Mom nodded, but she looked like she wished she hadn't agreed to it. I didn't like seeing Mom upset, but I couldn't *not* do things I liked to do, just to keep her from worrying about me all the time.

"Remember when I was younger, and I could walk better on my own?" I asked.

"Of course I do." Mom's coffee mug clinked on the table.

"So when I got to where I couldn't walk as well, I had to adapt. Like one way was to use the ramp you and Dad had built for me." I took a deep breath. "My disease is always changing, so I just have to learn to overcome whatever pops up next. You and Dad helped me with the ramp. But Charcot-Marie-Tooth is *my* disability, not yours."

Mom spoke in Chinese. I understood when she asked, "When did you get so smart?"

I laughed. "I'm a natural genius, I guess."

Mom laughed, too.

But you know what? She actually tried to help me brainstorm some ideas for my VP Club video. "Okay, so that one video you showed me was really good, Mia—the one where Saige finds a treasure beneath my rhododendron bushes. You made her look practically alive!"

Yeah, but that was just me pretending a doll could be a detective. This was something totally different. I needed something to sort of spotlight my video-making skills. You know, to show the judges I had real talent and that I'd make a great club president.

I guess Mom could tell I wasn't into her idea. "Have you talked to Ella about it?"

"Ella!" I smacked the table. "Why didn't I think of asking her already?" I held on to the edge of the table and walked around to hug Mom. "That's perfect. Thanks, Mom."

"You're welcome. But no texting Ella until you clean up your room first."

"Gotta go," I said, heading to my wheelchair so I could roll out of there fast.

Mom put her hands on her hips. "Mia, I'm serious."

Think my disability gets me out of doing chores? Not a chance. "I'm on it, Mom," I promised.

After I dusted my dresser, put away some clothes, and reorganized my desk, I reached for my phone.

Mia Lee: Help!

Then about five minutes later, my phone chimed. It was Ella.

Ella Lee: What's up?

Finally!

Mia Lee: So I definitely decided to run for Video Production Club president.

Ella Lee: Good 4 U! She sent a hand-clapping emoji.

Before I could respond, Ella texted again.

Ella Lee: So why do u need my help?

Mia Lee: B/c I need an idea for a campaign video.

No response. An hour later, still nothing. Thanks a lot for the help, Ella.

But that was okay. I could brainstorm on my own. I'd come up with some amazing ideas. Yeah, right. Twenty minutes later, my notebook was still perched on my lap. The only ink on the page was a couple of hearts I doodled in one corner.

"Knock, knock," Mom said, opening my door. "Would you like some company, Mia?"

"Maybe later, Mom." I never even looked away from my notebook. "But right now, I've got to come up with some ideas for the VP Club."

"That's why I'm here!" Caroline squealed. "I came over to help you with your campaign posters."

"Seriously?" I asked.

Caroline held up a box filled with art supplies. "Yep, your mom asked me if I could give you a hand. So of course, here I am."

I looked at Mom, surprised that she seemed to actually be coming around to the idea of my being in the VP Club.

Mom must've noticed because she said, "I thought about what you said earlier, Mia. I guess sometimes I forget that you do have interests that are all your own. And I forget how fast you're growing up." She came over to give me a hug. "I just want you to be happy. If that means running for VP Club president, then go for it."

I smiled. "Thanks, Mom."

"You're welcome. And I thought you might like having Caroline's input," Mom said.

I held up my notebook, filled with nothing but blank lines and two hearts. "Yeah, I need some help with this big time." Then I got an idea. "Hey, what if we get Rory and Daniela to come over, too?"

"Sure, I don't mind," Mom said.

For like half a second, I could've sworn Caroline frowned. So maybe she minded just a teensy bit. I asked her to make sure. "Is that cool with you, Caroline?"

She shrugged. "Um, yeah. It's your project, so it's fine with me."

"Awesome!" I texted Rory and Daniela, who came over in no time. Then we all sat around my room, working on my campaign posters.

I decided to give the superhero idea Caroline had suggested a few days ago a try. You know, it wasn't like I had any better ideas of my own. So Caroline copied pictures of my face and pasted it onto different superheroes' bodies. There was a poster of me as Wonder Woman and another of me as Captain America. My favorite was probably the one of me as Superman. I rocked the blue tights.

I came up with headings like *Want a SUPER VP Club? Vote Mia Lee for President* and *Mia Lee, Super VP President*. Rory and Daniela wrote my ideas on the posters in big block letters with markers. Then they glitterized them like crazy. Seriously. Red and blue glitter swirled all around my room.

"What d'ya think, Mia?" Caroline held up a poster of me as Batman.

I still wasn't totally sold on this superhero idea. I mean, I didn't exactly *feel* like a superhero because of my wheelchair. But we'd spent all afternoon working on these posters, and I couldn't have made them all by myself. I really, really appreciated all of the help. So I gave Caroline a thumbs-up and said, "It looks great!"

"It does," Rory agreed.

Daniela giggled. "You look super in a sparkly cape, Mia."

"Thanks, I think." I smiled.

Rory's mom stopped by to pick her up. Daniela was getting a ride with Rory, she also had to leave.

"I better go, too, Mia," Caroline said. "I'm revising my English paper."

"Geez, Louise!" I'd been so busy thinking about VP Club that I'd forgotten all about the English paper. It was due in a few days, too. Middle school had way too many deadlines, I'll tell you that.

After Caroline left, I grabbed my notebook again. I flipped the page over and wrote, *Mia Lee English Essay*. Then my phone chimed. Saved from my English homework by Ella.

Ella Lee: So sorry! Went to hang out with friends.

Mia Lee: No biggie.

Even though it sort of was.

Ella Lee: I feel bad tho. But I have a great idea for you.

Ella's great idea came a little too late. Because now, there were posters drying all over my room. Still, what did she come up with?

Mia Lee: So spill it!

Ella Lee: Be true to YOU.

What was that supposed to even mean? Now that Ella was in college, she said weird stuff sometimes. Half the time, I wasn't so sure Ella even knew what that stuff really meant. Her great idea wasn't so great after all. Really, it was junk.

I thanked Ella and told her goodnight. The whole time I was trying to go to sleep, all I could think about was Ella's text, though. Be true to me. What did that mean?

...

The next morning, Miss Jackson met me at my bus.

"Mia, look at your campaign posters!" she said, reaching for the poster boards to carry them inside the school. "These are great!"

"Thanks," I said. "I had lots of help, though."

Caroline, Rory, and Daniela didn't just show up at my house yesterday to help me make my posters. They also helped me hang them up at school today. "You guys are the best!" I said when we hung the last poster near our table inside the lunchroom.

"Best friends!" Rory said, putting her hand out.

Daniela smiled and put her hand on top of Rory's. "Best friends!"

"Best friends!" I said, putting my hand in, too.

We waited. When Caroline didn't put her hand in because she was busy wiping it off on her jeans, I nudged her.

"Sorry," she said. "Stinking glitter." She finally put her hand on top of mine.

Then we all raised our hands up toward the ceiling and laughed. I'd never had three best friends before. And you know, I liked it. I mean, Caroline was still my number one *best* best friend of course. But it was fun hanging out with Rory and Daniela, too.

Only, we didn't laugh for long after that because there came Angela.

"You're kidding me, right? You really think you're a superhero?" Angela was the only one laughing now.

Well, make that Angela *and* Jess. "Yeah, that's hilarious," Jess agreed, giggling.

"You left out one superhero, though." Angela made a pouty face, like she was disappointed.

When I didn't say anything, Angela went on. "Super Klutz. Remember?"

How could I forget? Angela called me Super Klutz on the very first day of school. I felt a little hot tear trying to bubble up out of my eye, but I held it in tight. Because no matter what, I refused to cry in front of Angela. Nope. Not happening.

"Guess what, Angela?" I finally said. "If I was a superhero, *Poof!* I'd make you disappear right now."

Angela frowned. "That's so lame. And you better be nice to me, or I might not even let you join the VP Club when *I* become president." She shrugged. "Face it, you're so gonna lose the election. I'll make sure of it."

Wow! Angela was super, too—super mean, that is! I couldn't believe I'd been dumb enough to actually think she and I could ever have been friends.

"Forget her," Caroline said when Angela and Jess walked away.

"Yeah," Rory said. "Don't even listen to Angela."

I nodded. They were right. I had to ignore Angela and stay focused on my campaign video. But I couldn't shake the last thing Angela said about her making sure I lose.

At lunchtime, I knew Angela meant it.

"My poster!" I cried. "It's gone!"

Rory whirled around in her seat. "Hey, it is!"

"I know we hung one there," Daniela chimed in.

"We did, for sure," I said. "It was the one of me as Captain America."

Caroline came over with her tray. "Hey, guys!" She smiled. "What's up?"

"Well," I began, "I can tell you what's not up—my campaign poster." I pointed to the white block wall where we'd hung my poster earlier. No poster, no tape, no nothing.

Caroline didn't say anything, but we'd been best friends long enough that she didn't have to. I knew Caroline was just as upset as I was.

"So any guesses on who took it?" I asked.

Caroline pulled out her chicken wrap. "Uh—" she began.

"That's right. Angela," I finished for her. "And I'm going to prove she stole my poster."

"How?" Rory gulped.

"I'm not sure," I said. "But don't worry. We won't get into trouble or anything."

Rory looked relieved.

At least I didn't think we would. But just in case, I tried crossing my fingers.

Chapter Eleven: Poster Thief On The Loose

"Hang on, Mia," Daniela said, biting into a pickle. "What if it's not Angela?"

Had Daniela lost it? Of course it was Angela. "Who else would it be? She even said she'd make sure I lost the VP election," I reminded her.

"Right." Daniela nodded. "But I saw Blake Lyle hanging up some campaign posters. He's running for VP Club president, too."

Geez, Louise! I'd been so busy worrying about Angela that I didn't even think about any other competition.

"So who is Blake Lyle anyway?" Rory asked.

"I know who he is," I said. "He wears red glasses. His hair does this wave kind of thing over his right eye. Every day, he smells like sweaty spaghetti."

Rory laughed. "You know a lot about him, Mia." She wiggled her eyebrows up and down and sang, "Must be a middle school cru-ush."

I stuck out my tongue. "Who crushes on sweaty spaghetti?"

"True," Rory agreed. "But you do seem to know a lot about Blake."

"Well," I began, "he is in my music class. And I have a Blake file saved in my brain."

"What about me?" Daniela tapped on my head. "Is there a Daniela file in here?"

I nodded. "Yep. I logged it when you sneaked an extra packet of honey mustard sauce the first time we ate lunch together."

Daniela looked surprised. "You saw that?"

I laughed. "Yep."

"Oops. Sorry." She grinned. "But you know how I am about honey mustard."

"We do now." Rory smiled, too.

Then Daniela got all serious again. She took a big huffy breath and folded her arms across her chest, like we were really trying her patience. "But you're missing a piece of the file, Mia. Blake hangs out with the kids who were picking on me in English class last week."

"Seriously?" I asked. Blake hung out with the Boy Bullies and their leader, Mr. McBully?

T-W Middle was a big school. I still didn't know everyone yet or which kids hung out in which groups. So Daniela was right. I didn't really know who Blake's friends were.

Daniela nodded. "After you stuck up for me, they probably don't want you to win this election. Who knows? Maybe Blake and his friends are taking down your posters."

First, Angela. Now, Blake. I shrugged. "Maybe I should just drop out. It's not like I'll win anyway."

"No way!" Rory said.

"You can't quit." Daniela said. "Right, Caroline?"

Caroline was pretty quiet all through lunch. I thought she was really starting to like Rory and Daniela, too. But today, it was like I got a whole different vibe.

Daniela waved her hand in front of Caroline's face. "Caroline? Yoo-hoo!"

When Caroline still didn't say anything, I asked, "Are you okay?"

"Sure," Caroline said. "Why wouldn't I be?"

"Just checking," I said. With homework and the VP Club election, Caroline and I hadn't talked as much lately, except when everyone was at my house yesterday. We had to get together, just the two of us, to hang out soon.

Now Rory and Daniela wrapped napkins around their straws. They even wrote "Go, Mia!" on them and waved them in the air like little flags. They made one for Caroline, too.

"You're all crazy!" I laughed. Then I said, "Okay, I won't drop out."

"Yay!" Rory said.

"But," I went on, "I am going to find out what Blake Lyle is up to."

"Then what are you waiting for?" Daniela asked. "Let's go."

After lunch, I went with Rory and Daniela to the gym. We tried to talk Caroline into coming with us, but she wanted to work on her English paper again. That seemed like all she did anymore. Anyway, Daniela said Blake hung out down at the gym sometimes before the bell rang. That was exactly where we were headed.

At first, I didn't see Blake because apparently lots of boys went to the gym after lunch. The place was packed, and basketballs bounced all around.

"There he is," I said when I finally spotted him. Sure enough, Blake was shooting hoops with the boys who'd picked on Daniela about her *Doctor Who* T-shirt.

"He doesn't look as mean as they do," Rory said.

She was right. Blake didn't look that mean. We'd even talked a little bit in music class. He seemed pretty cool. I was usually right about that kind of stuff. But hey, because Blake hung out with those three jerks, maybe I was wrong this time.

While we watched them play basketball, I updated Blake's file in my head.

Hobby: Basketball

Talent: Sweats hearts

That's because, no joke, there was a heart-shaped sweat stain on his T-shirt. It was gross but impressive.

The ball bounced out of bounds and straight toward us. Daniela grabbed it.

"Hey, give us that ball back," Mr. McBully said. "We don't want your freak-o germs on it."

The other boys laughed. Then one said, "What was on her shirt again? Oh yeah, I got it: *Doctor Poo.*" That really got them going, like seriously, almost rolling on the hardwood floor. Boys could be superlame sometimes.

I updated the Boy Bullies file, too. I stamped *Even Meaner than Mean! Mean! Mean!* all over it.

"I don't get it," Blake said. "What's so funny?"

Then the other boys told Blake all about Daniela's *Doctor Who* shirt. One of them said, "And supposedly that girl"—he pointed at me—"knows martial arts, but I don't buy it for a second."

"Me neither," Mr. McBully said, staring at my legs as if he was trying to figure out why I wore braces. Then he asked, "What's wrong with your legs anyway?"

"Marcus!" Blake said.

Marcus, huh? So now I knew the bully leader's name. Marcus McBully had a nice ring to it.

"It's okay," I finally said, and it really was. I got that question all the time, so I was used to it.

I didn't get to answer Marcus's question about my legs, though, because Blake started talking about my stop-motion videos.

"I wouldn't mess with Mia if I were you," Blake told the other boys. "My sister says her videos are super popular online."

"So?" Marcus said.

"So she might make Hollywood movies someday," Blake said. "Then she would name all of her bad guys Marcus."

"You're kidding, right?" Marcus said.

"Nope." Blake shook his head. "Every last one of them, even the evil stepmothers."

Now that was funny. All of us laughed except the Boy Bullies. They went back to shooting hoops after that.

But I didn't come to the gym to talk about Hollywood movies or evil stepmothers. I came to check up on Blake because of the Video Production Club. Even if he was nice just now, Blake was still my competition. I wondered what he knew. "So you're running for VP Club president, too, huh?"

"Yep. Me, you, and Angela. I heard some other kid was running, too. The video competition should be fierce."

"I think it already is," I said.

Blake looked confused. "What d'ya mean?"

"Someone is stealing my campaign posters," I said.

"Who would do that?" Blake asked.

Rory got in on it then. "That's what we're wondering, too."

"Let me know if you find out who's doing it," Blake said. "I don't want anybody stealing mine." Then he looked at the basketball Daniela still held. "Can I have that back please?"

"Oh, sorry." Daniela bounced it to him.

Then Blake said, "See ya!" before dribbling the ball back across the gym.

"He didn't do it," I said.

"Are you sure?" Daniela still didn't look convinced.

"Positive," I said. I could tell when somebody was lying. They fidgeted and wouldn't look me in the eye, but Blake didn't do any of that. He might be guilty of hanging out with some jerks, but Blake didn't touch my posters.

Suddenly, Caroline came running into the gym. "Mia!" she said. "Didn't you hang a poster in the hall next to the library, too?"

I nodded. "It was my Wonder Woman poster. Let me guess, it's gone, too?"

"Yep," Caroline said.

Rory frowned. "Why would anybody do this to you?"

"I don't know," I said.

With the election only a few days away, I didn't have much time left to figure this all out. Who was stealing my campaign posters and why?

Chapter Twelve:
One, Two, Three, Best Friends!

On Wednesday evening, Rory invited Caroline, Daniela, and me over to her house to meet Roofus. With only a couple of days left until we turned in our English essays, Rory got this great idea for us to share our opening paragraphs. A sneak peek preview, she'd called it.

I'd never been to Rory's house before. Mom helped me to the door and rang the doorbell. A lady wearing a Kiss the Cook apron met us at the door. She had pink, round cheeks, just like Rory.

"Welcome! I'm Karen, Rory's mom." After she shook hands with my mom, she turned to me. "You must be Mia. I just took a batch of chocolate chip cookies out of the oven for you girls to snack on."

"My favorite." I smiled. Karen seemed nice. Plus, I liked that she didn't make a big deal out of my braces. She acted like I was a regular kid, just like the other girls.

"Mine, too," Karen said. "Come on in. Rory and the other girls are waiting for you."

So I was the last one to show. As soon as the others heard me come in, Rory came running over. "Mia!" She gave me a hug. Roofus started barking.

"Hi, Rory! Hey, Roofus!" I said, giving him a pat behind his ears. "You're right, Rory. He is adorable."

"Told you," she said. "Let's go downstairs."

So I told Mom bye, and Rory led us all to the basement. Caroline and Daniela went ahead, while Rory waited for me. I held on to the rail and took the stairs real slow, one at a time.

Downstairs, Rory took us over to a set of couches. "I can't wait to hear everyone's essays," she began. "Who wants to go first?"

"I will, I guess," Daniela said. She opened up her notebook and read, "The Middle Child by Daniela Rodriguez. Dear Reader, being the middle child really stinks. I have two older brothers and two younger sisters. I love them a lot, but sometimes it feels like nobody in my family really understands me. My parents are from Mexico, and they don't understand why I love *Doctor Who* and American things. At school, I'm not popular, and I don't fit in. I just wish I knew more people who were more like me."

We were all quiet for a second, like none of us knew what to say. I mean, I hadn't watched *Doctor Who* before, and I wasn't a middle child. Still, I did get some of what Daniela said.

"My parents are from China," I finally said. "Sometimes they don't understand the things I like either. Like they think the pop music I listen to is silly. They don't really get my stop-motion videos, honestly, or any of the videos I watch online. And trust me"—I pointed to my braces—"I hear you about not fitting in. But you fit in here." I nodded toward Caroline and Rory.

Daniela smiled. "Thanks, Mia."

"Next!" Rory said. Boy, she was really good at this meeting stuff.

"I guess I'll go," Caroline spoke up. She didn't look at anyone as she started to read, "My Fault by Caroline Zaler. My mom and dad got a divorce when I was in fourth grade. In fifth grade, my dad moved to Florida. I was really sad because now I could only see him during vacations. This summer, when I went to Florida, I met his new family. My stepmother is really pretty, and I have a new stepsister. I guess I'm happy that he's happy, and they're really nice. But I wonder if it's my fault he left, and if he's going to like his new family more than he likes me now."

No way! I knew Caroline was superupset when her dad left, but I had no clue she thought her parents' divorce was her fault or that her dad wouldn't love her anymore.

I leaned over and hugged Caroline. "I wish I knew this before," I said. "You can always tell me anything. You know that, right?"

Caroline nodded.

I got the feeling there was something else she wanted to say, but then Rory said, "Ahem," and began, "Being Me by Rory Thomas. Have you ever pretended you were someone else? I have for my whole life. My mom wants me to be super smart in school, just like she was. She even made me join the debate team. Truth? I'm not a brainiac. And what I really want to do is train Roofus for dog shows. I've already taught him tons of tricks. Mom just hasn't noticed."

Daniela was the first to speak up. "That's so sad!"

Caroline shot Rory a sympathetic look. "Have you told your mom about the stuff *you* like?"

Rory looked down. "Not lately."

"Maybe you should let her know you're not into the debate team," Daniela said. "Tell her what you just told us about training Roofus."

"That's a good idea," I chimed in.

"Maybe I will." Rory sounded more confident now.

Now I sort of understood why Rory was a teacher's pet. She tried really, really hard to make everyone else happy, starting with her mom.

"So," Daniela said, "what about you, Mia? What's your story?"

"About that"—I held up my blank notebook—"I kind of don't have one yet."

"What? You have only two days until it's due!" Rory freaked a little.

I nodded. "Yeah, I get that. I just haven't had anything to write about." Then I smiled. "Until now."

The other girls' stories, they were super personal. They made me think about being in the gym a couple of days ago and how Marcus McBully asked what was wrong with my legs. So I grabbed my notebook, and I wrote. It was everything I wanted to say to Marcus that day but didn't. And everything I've ever wanted to say to other kids like Angela and to adults, too.

For the first time in my life, writing words on paper was easy. I mean, it still took forever because I kept dropping my pencil. But I finally had a story—my story. That was even what I wrote for my title.

"Here goes," I said when I finished writing. "My Story by Mia Lee. Sometimes, I get sick of the stares and the questions. 'What's wrong with her?' they whisper. Guess what? Just because my legs and hands don't work the same as most people's, my ears still do. On the outside, people see Charcot-Marie-Tooth disease. But on the inside, I am Mia Lee. I really like making cool stop-motion videos. I like creating cartoons with my best friend, Caroline. I like hanging out with my new friends, too, laughing and having fun. I'm totally normal, just like you."

"Mia, we all know you're normal," Rory said, giving me a big hug. Then Caroline and Daniela piled in for one big group hug.

I smiled. "Thanks."

Caroline teased, "Except for when you eat the very last chocolate chip cookie. That's not so normal."

I laughed. Caroline was talking about the plate of cookies Rory's mom had baked for us earlier. We'd munched on them while we worked. "Sorry, but they were *so* good!" Then I said, "Hey, I've got it!"

"Wait! First, you must promise you shall not eat the last cookie ever again," Daniela teased, too.

"Never!" I joked. "But see, I haven't gotten any ideas for my campaign video for VP Club. What if I do a stop-motion video about my disability?" Why didn't I think of that before? Plus, I was taking Mr. Postin's advice about choosing a topic that really mattered to me.

"Like what?" Rory asked. "Don't stop-motions have to have dolls in them?"

"Nope, they don't have to." I looked at Caroline and smiled. "I'm picturing a cartoon stop-motion." I filled her in on my Mean Middle School Monster idea and asked, "Can you help me?"

Caroline smiled. "Sure!"

"What if you're the superhero, like your posters?" Rory suggested.

"Hey, I love that idea. Except," I said, "instead of having a superhero body, it'll just be me, you know, the *real* Mia Lee."

"And you can battle the Mean Middle School Monster with your superhero powers," Daniela chimed in.

Suddenly, the ideas were pouring in. Caroline, Rory, and Daniela wrote down most of them. Then I thought of something else.

"The campaign videos have to be turned in on Friday, guys," I said. "How will I ever be able to write an entire comic in two days?"

"We'll all help you," Caroline said, "won't we?"

Rory and Daniela agreed.

"Hey, I got an even better idea. Since it's my story, why don't I narrate it as the comics flash on the screen? Then it'll be my real voice telling my real story." So maybe Mom was right. Maybe I really did have a story hiding inside of me after all. But instead of writing it all out on paper, my story is a video.

"I love it!" Daniela said.

So we jotted down a few more ideas until it was time to go home. Before we left, Rory held out her hand and said, "Bring it in."

Then we all put our hands in the middle. On the count of three, we said, "Best friends!" and raised our hands in the air. That was sort of becoming our thing.

On the way home, I texted Ella. I told her all about my campaign video and about hanging out with my friends. Middle school was awesome—finally!

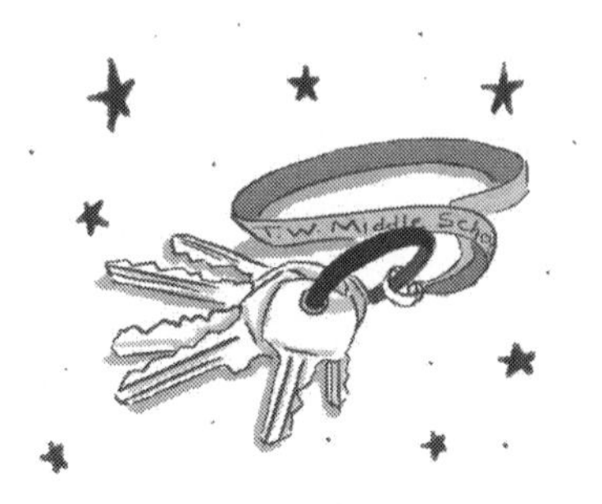

Chapter Thirteen: Locker Burglar

Friday was a super busy day, starting with English class.

"Everybody, please take out your self-description essays," Ms. Randells announced. Then she flitted around the room collecting papers.

I pulled out my English folder, smoothed out my essay, and handed it to Ms. Randells. I couldn't keep from smiling when she read my title and said, "Thank you, Mia. I look forward to reading your story."

My story—that made me sound like a real writer. When Ms. Randells gave us this essay assignment on the first day of school, I was clueless, like I didn't even know where to start.

But once I found a topic that really mattered to me, the writing got easier. Finishing my essay was a breeze. I know, right? Me, Mia Lee, the terrible writer. Who knows? Maybe I wasn't so terrible anymore. Someday, I might even win an essay contest like Ella.

After English class, the rest of the day was one giant blur. That was because I was so excited. It was almost time to go home. But first, I had to turn in my VP campaign video.

"So you've gotta go with me to give my DVD to Mr. Postin," I said to Caroline, Rory, and Daniela.

"Sure!" Caroline said, readjusting her backpack. We all headed down the hall to Mr. Postin's classroom.

"I think you have a really, really good shot at winning this competition," Rory said.

I shrugged. "I don't know."

"Well, we do," Daniela chimed in. "Your video is amazing, Mia."

I grinned. "Thanks, Daniela. I couldn't have finished it without your help."

That was true. Caroline spent tons of time drawing the cartoons. Rory helped me pick out the music to put with the graphics. Daniela helped me edit everything and burn it onto a DVD. I had never done a cartoon stop-motion before, but I was really proud of how it turned out. I even posted it online along with my other stop-motion videos.

I thanked them again for all their help and said, "You guys are awesome!"

"We are pretty awesome, aren't we?" Daniela joked.

We all laughed.

"Awesome? Or *awful*?" Apparently, Angela was headed to turn in her campaign video, too. And just our luck, we ran into her and Jess.

She held up her DVD. "Here's the winner."

Angela's DVD looked professional. She'd even made a pink cover that said "Angela Vanover Productions" in fancy gold cursive writing. Mine just said "Mia Lee" in plain black Sharpie.

"I wouldn't count on it," Rory said.

Angela laughed. "I already know I'll get more votes." She tossed her hair over one shoulder. "More people saw my campaign posters than yours. That's because yours never stuck around for long." Then she looked at Jess. "Get it? *Stuck* around, like stuck to the walls."

"Good one, Ang!" Jess laughed, too. "Those superhero posters were just dumb anyways."

"Tell me about it!" Angela shook her head. "See ya, Super K!" Then they hurried ahead of us to Mr. Postin's classroom.

"Super K?" Daniela asked. "That doesn't even make any sense."

But it did to me: Super Klutz. I couldn't change Angela's mind about my being a klutz, but hopefully my campaign video would.

"Here you go, Mr. Postin," I said when we reached his desk.

Mr. Postin looked up from a stack of papers he was grading. "Thank you, Mia." He placed my DVD right on top of Angela's and then handed me a sheet of paper. "Here is Monday's election day schedule. Look it over, and let me know if you have any questions."

Video Production Club Election Day

3:00 p.m. Candidate Video Presentations

4:00 p.m. Election Results

4:30 p.m. Snacks

"Nope, I think I've got it," I said.

"Great." Mr. Postin smiled. "On Monday, the other judges and I will view the videos and award points. Then we'll share them with the entire club at our meeting Monday afternoon. Once we tally the votes, we'll announce our new VP Club president."

"So that's how it all works, huh?"

"That's it in a nutshell." Mr. Postin smiled again. "Have a nice weekend, Mia."

"You, too, Mr. Postin," I said, wheeling myself back out into the hallway. But then I stopped. "Where's Caroline?"

"Hey," Rory said. "She's still hanging out around Mr. Postin's desk."

"Caroline, we're leaving," I called.

"Earth to Caroline," Daniela said in this weird alien voice.

Rory laughed. I would've, too, except I was sort of getting worried about Caroline. She was acting stranger than usual, even for her.

When Rory and Daniela left to grab their bus seats home, I decided to talk to her about it.

"What's up, Caroline?"

"Nothing. Why?" She looked at me as if I was the one with a problem.

"You're just different lately, is all."

Caroline shifted her backpack. When she did, something fell out and clattered to the tile floor. She scrambled to grab it and shoved it back into her backpack.

"Is that a CD?" I asked. "I thought you downloaded your music."

"Uh, yeah."

"The gold writing on it was sort of like Angela's DVD," I said. That was weird—not the gold writing part but that Caroline bought a CD. Only my dad still buys CDs.

Caroline didn't say anything.

"Maybe I can come over to listen to it," I said.

"Listen to what?" Caroline looked confused.

"Your new CD, silly," I reminded her. "It's been a while since you and I hung out, just the two of us. So we should—soon."

"Seriously?"

I didn't get why Caroline looked so surprised, but she smiled and shot me a thumbs-up. "Yeah, we should. But right now, I've got some stuff I need to do. See ya later," Caroline said, disappearing around some lockers.

"Mia!" Miss Jackson came up behind me. "I've been looking everywhere for you."

"Sorry. I had to give my campaign video to Mr. Postin."

Miss Jackson patted my shoulder. "It's okay. You've gotten a lot more independent now that you're in middle school." She laughed. "It's hard for me to keep up with you."

I smiled. I hadn't really thought about it, but I sort of was more independent.

"So listen," Miss Jackson began, "I've got to run to the teacher's lounge. I'll be right back to get you settled on your bus. Wait right here, okay?"

"You got it," I said.

I got tired of sitting in the same spot, so I rolled myself a little farther down the hallway. When I did, though, something jingled. It turned out, Miss J had hung her sweater on my wheelchair handle and her lanyard that held all of her keys, too.

I reached for the keys and plopped them in my lap. I stared at them. I mean, here were the keys Miss Jackson told me unlocked practically every T-W Middle School lock there was. And everybody else have pretty much left already to catch their buses home. I still hadn't figured out for sure who was taking my posters, and now I could.

Plus, I'd made some thank-you cards for Caroline, Rory, and Daniela for helping me with my VP Club video. So now was the perfect time to slide them in their lockers, which I did, one at a time. Rory's locker was first, then Daniela's.

Caroline's was all the way down at the end of the hall. I tried to squeeze the card through the slats, but it was harder than Rory's and Daniela's had been. I sort of shoved it to make it fit. When I did so, Miss J's keys tumbled out of my lap and onto the floor.

"Geez, Louise!" I muttered. "Get back here, keys." I swiped at the lanyard. That was when I noticed the sparkles on the floor. I'd never noticed the red and blue specks swirled in with the black tile. "Wait a minute," I half whispered. That was because the red and blue specks weren't just on the floor anymore. They were also on my fingers where I'd grabbed the keys and on Miss J's lanyard, too.

Then I remembered something. Those red and blue sparkles, they were the same color as the glitter on my superhero posters. But why would they be here, right next to Caroline's locker? I logged into my Brain Files to try to figure it out.

Subject: Red and blue glitter

Last Seen: On my VP campaign posters

Location: Found next to Caroline's locker of all places!

Still Unknown: Who put them there?

I got a sinking feeling then. Angela was trying to frame Caroline. She took my VP campaign posters and tried to make it look like Caroline did it. This was definitely a crime scene. I pulled out my cell and snapped a few pictures for evidence. I bet if I looked, there'd be glitter outside of Angela's locker, too.

I pushed myself back down the hall. Finding Angela's locker was easy. Hers was the only one with a star sticker on the door. I scanned the floor—not one speck of glitter. But what if Angela cleaned up the evidence already? What if my campaign posters were in her locker right now?

I reached for Miss J's keys again. All I had to do was slide the locker key into Angela's lock, and I'd know if Angela took my posters and stashed them in there. But as usual, my fingers wouldn't move the way I wanted them to. I couldn't make them grab the key I needed.

"Hey! Get away from my locker!"

Uh-oh. Angela.

"Mia!" said Miss Jackson. "What are you doing?" She snatched her keys away from me.

That was a good question. What was I doing? I wasn't sure. I mean, I didn't actually even touch Angela's locker. But I thought about it. I'd almost turned into the locker burglar Miss J warned me about last week. No kidding.

Chapter Fourteen: True Burglar...True Friend?

Just like that, I thought the whole thing with me at Angela's locker was old news. But first thing on Monday morning at school, I found out it wasn't.

Miss J pushed me down the hallway to homeroom. I was texting Ella to thank her for the "Good luck with your VP election!" text she'd sent when Caroline, Rory, and Daniela rushed over.

Rory pointed and said, "Mia, look."

"Hey, my poster is back," I said. It was the one of me as Wonder Woman. Maybe Angela felt bad for stealing my posters, or maybe she was scared she'd get caught. It didn't matter. At least she'd done the right thing and finally returned it.

When Angela walked past, I said, "Thanks."

She frowned. "What are you talking about?"

I couldn't say anything else because Mr. Postin came out into the hall then. Blake and Judson Goldstein, the other kid who was running for VP Club president, were with him. Mr. Postin asked us all to come to his classroom. He didn't look happy at all. I got a feeling that something was up, something big.

"It seems we have a slight issue," Mr. Postin began. "I personally collected campaign videos from all of our candidates on Friday afternoon. However, today, there are only three for our committee to view. One DVD is missing."

I'd always heard about it being so quiet you could hear a pin drop. Now I got how quiet that was.

It was probably my video that was missing. Angela took it, just like my posters. But wait a minute. Angela returned my posters, or one of them at least. So why do something nice, and then steal my DVD instead? It didn't add up.

"Angela," Mr. Postin said, "I'm sorry to say, your video is missing."

"What? No way!" she wailed.

"Calm down." Mr. Postin folded his hands across his big belly and glanced at his watch. "I know you turned in a DVD. Given the circumstances, the committee and I will allow you to submit another copy or send us a link to the video."

"I know who took it," Angela said.

Mr. Postin's eyebrows shot up above his glasses. "You do?"

Angela pointed at me. "It was Mia. She took it."

All eyes were on me now.

"After school on Friday, I saw Mia snooping around outside my locker," Angela went on. "She stole her aide's keys. And she was going to steal my stuff, too. Mia's a thief."

What? Angela was the one stealing my posters, and now she was accusing me of stealing her video? I almost could've laughed then, except, you know, everyone was still staring at me. I didn't like being accused of something I didn't do.

"I don't know what to say," Mr. Postin said, but he looked at Miss J then. "If you can shed some light on this situation, please do."

"What Angela is saying about Mia having my keys is true," Miss Jackson said. "But she didn't steal my keys. I left them on the back of her wheelchair while I ran to the teacher's lounge. That was an error on my part."

Geez, Louise! I never thought about Miss J getting into trouble. How did I fix this? There was only one way—to come clean. "But that wasn't your fault, Miss Jackson," I finally said. "I was the one who snatched your keys. That was my fault, not yours. Please don't fire Miss J."

"No one is getting fired here," Mr. Postin said. "But please explain yourself, Mia. Were you, as Angela says, 'snooping' around her locker?"

I swallowed hard and then told everyone about my missing posters and how I thought Angela was stealing them. I left out the part about why, though.

But Rory and Daniela didn't. They told everyone that Angela called me Super Klutz, plus all the mean things she'd said to me.

"Honestly, it wasn't me!" Angela said. "I didn't take Mia's posters." She lowered her voice. "But I guess I was sort of mean."

"Sort of?" I said.

Angela shrugged. "Okay, a lot. And I'm sorry. It's just, I saw your stop-motion videos online. I never get four hundred likes on my makeup tutorials."

My videos online? Did Angela post videos, too? I knew I had seen her face somewhere—probably one of her makeup tutorials.

"Your videos are really good, so I knew you'd probably win this competition," Angela went on. "And I knew my mom would be super disappointed in me if I lost." Angela's voice got really soft when she said, "It's like she expects me to be perfect. Sometimes, I can't take the pressure."

I wasn't really sure what to say to that. So I just sort of nodded. I mean, I'd seen Angela's mom in action. She *was* really pushy. I got what it's like to have a pushy mom, except my mom was only pushy sometimes because she worried about my health. Angela's mom seemed more worried about looks, winning, and stuff like that.

I even felt sort of sorry for Angela. Now I was sure about one thing: Angela didn't take my posters.

"So let me get this straight," Mr. Postin said. "Mia, you thought Angela was stealing your campaign posters?"

I nodded.

"But you really didn't. Right, Angela?" Mr. Postin said.

"Right," Angela agreed.

"But now you think Mia stole your DVD. Correct?"

Angela looked at me. "I'm not sure."

"I promise, I didn't take it," I said.

"Then who did?" Mr. Postin asked. "Blake? Judson? You two have been awfully quiet. Do either of you have anything to say about this?"

I didn't know who looked more surprised, Blake or Judson, but they both shook their heads.

Mr. Postin sighed. "I believe we should postpone this afternoon's VP election until we get to the bottom of this."

I raised my hand. "Mr. Postin?"

"Yes, Mia."

"I think I know who did this." I bit my lip and glanced toward Caroline, Rory, and Daniela. "But what I don't know is why."

My brain pulled up a file. I wished I could click Cancel or hit Delete, or even better, force a shut down. But I couldn't.

Subject: Someone I never suspected—until now

Talents: Highly skilled in horse snorts and neighing sounds

A.K.A.: My BFF

Evidence: Red and blue glitter that matched my VP posters outside her locker. And she never buys CDs—ever.

"I think it was Caroline." I turned toward her then. "But *why* did you take my posters, Caroline? And Angela's DVD?"

Rory and Daniela's mouths dropped open. Caroline wouldn't even look at me. She fiddled with the zipper on her backpack.

"Caroline, is this true?" Mr. Postin asked.

Caroline slowly nodded.

Mr. Postin had the same question as me. "Why, Caroline?"

"Because," Caroline began, "Mia is my best friend. But now she's hanging out with Rory and Daniela, too." She looked at me, and tears rolled down her cheeks. "I was afraid you were like my dad. He left when he found somebody he liked better than my mom. And I thought you wouldn't be my best friend anymore, now that you found some girls you liked better."

Caroline wasn't just making all this up. I knew she was for real because of the essay she wrote about her dad. But I was sad that my best friend thought I'd ever ditch her for somebody else.

"So I took Mia's posters, hoping she wouldn't win the election," Caroline went on. "That way, she wouldn't make even more friends. And she'd still hang out with me."

"But why did you take my DVD?" Angela asked.

"Because on Friday, Mia said we could hang out together, just the two of us. And then I knew I was being silly." Caroline wiped away tears with the back of her hand. "So I got her posters out of my locker and hung them back up. I was afraid I'd made Mia lose the election already. And I thought taking your DVD would, you know, fix things."

"But instead, things got even worse," Mr. Postin said.

Caroline nodded.

"So that's why there was glitter around your locker. And why you said you had stuff to do on Friday?" I asked. "And I thought a CD fell out of your backpack in the hall. It really was Angela's DVD, wasn't it?"

Caroline took a big breath and nodded again. "I'm sorry," she said. Then Caroline reached into her backpack and pulled out Angela's DVD. "Here. And if it makes a difference, I'd already decided to give it back. Before all this happened, I mean. I couldn't even sleep all weekend. I'm really sorry."

At first, I didn't think Angela was going to accept her apology. But when she took her DVD from Caroline, she said, "It's okay, Caroline. I do dumb stuff sometimes, too."

Caroline looked relieved. Then she came over to me. "I hope you don't hate me, Mia. I'm really, really sorry." She sniffed.

I held on to my chair and stood up to hug Caroline. "Taking my stuff and Angela's stuff was really, really dumb. But best friends don't hate each other."

"I made a humongo mess," Caroline said.

I patted her shoulder. "Yeah, you did. But I make humongo messes, too, like with the scavenger hunt photos and taking Miss J's keys."

That reminded me that I had some apologizing of my own to do. So I came clean with Mr. Postin about the day I stopped by his classroom, too. "I'd hoped you'd accidentally spill some information on how to score VP Club video points for the election. And when you didn't, I decided just to ask you. But you still wouldn't tell."

Mr. Postin smiled. "I already knew."

"You did?" I asked.

"Absolutely! When you've been a teacher for as long as I have, you learn to read students quite well. *And* you know when to give extra assignments when students misbehave. Speaking of which, here you go, Caroline." Mr. Postin gave her a whole folder full of extra math worksheets. "I want these turned in before the end of this week. You will also have plenty of time to think about your actions while you spend a couple of days after school in detention. Understand?"

"Yes, sir," Caroline said.

Then I apologized to Miss Jackson and ended with, "You're the best aide I've ever had."

Miss J hugged me. "And you're the best student I've ever had, Mia." Then she smiled. "I'll just have to watch my keys around you from now on."

I laughed even though I was never ever going to touch Miss J's keys again.

So now we knew who took my posters and Angela's DVD. But there was still one question left to answer. Who would be our new VP Club president?

Chapter Fifteen: A V.P. Club Victory

After school, everyone headed to the library for the VP Club election. Four chairs were lined in a row at the front of the room and labeled with our names: Judson, Angela, Mia, and Blake.

Mr. Postin got the video presentations rolling. Judson's video was first, and it highlighted him and his buddies' fancy footwork on the soccer field. The best part was the hip-hop background music. I bopped around in my seat.

For Angela's video, she interviewed Main Street business owners, like she was some news reporter. They talked about some things going on downtown to revive the area, like a new ice cream shop set to open soon.

"Yum!" I whispered to Angela. She smiled.

My video was next. I was nervous now. I mean, so far, mine was the only one that was really personal. It was sort of like I'd opened my diary and shared it with the world, except in a video.

But there was no stopping it when "Super Mia Lee" popped up on the screen. And there was Caroline's cartoon of me in my wheelchair. I wore a cape and a mask. I used my crazy superhero skills to end the Mean Middle School Monster's madness.

I couldn't take my eyes off the screen the whole time. The last scene ended with, "The real Mia Lee is a normal kid, except she makes supercool stop-motion videos. And, oh yeah, she has Charcot-Marie-Tooth. So look out! She can beat you in a wheelchair race. And she pops the occasional wheelie."

Okay, that last line was a stretch. I couldn't pop wheelies on my own. But when my dad was home, he made riding in this wheelchair fun—for real.

Everybody started clapping. Blake leaned over and said, "That was cool!"

"Yeah, but I know the Mean Middle School Monster is me," Angela said.

Uh-oh. Was she mad?

"I'm sorry for acting like such a brat," Angela said. "No excuse or anything. But I just didn't know why you're in a wheelchair or why you drop stuff a lot."

"That's okay," I said, and it really was. Lots of people didn't know about muscular dystrophy. Now everybody in this room did at least. It was sappy, but no matter who was elected VP Club president, I was still super proud of my video.

Blake's video was last. He shot lots of footage around T-W Middle. Students and staff talked about why they loved our school. Blake's graphics exploded off the screen. They were amazing, like the best I'd seen.

"Ladies and gentlemen," Mr. Postin said, "please help yourselves to some snacks while we tally the votes. We'll have the results shortly."

Miss J brought my wheelchair over. She helped me over to the snack table. I grabbed a cheese sandwich and some apple slices. Rory pushed me over to the table where she and Daniela were sitting.

When Caroline came over with her plate, she had tuna on wheat and carrot sticks.

"How will you survive without your usual chicken wrap?" I teased.

Caroline shrugged. "I figured sometimes trying something new seems scary at first, but it turns out to be really amazing."

"You mean like hanging out with us?" Daniela smiled.

Caroline licked her lips. "No, I mean like carrot sticks dunked in ranch dressing." Then she laughed. "Of course, like hanging out with you guys. But these carrots aren't so bad either." She looked at me. "Why didn't you ever tell me?"

"Since when do you listen to me, partner?" I asked. Then I slung an imaginary lasso. "Yee-haw!"

Caroline died laughing. Then she said, "Wait a minute. I did listen to you. And you said we couldn't do that now that we're in middle school. We have to be cool. Remember?"

"Did I say that?" I pretended to think about it. Then I smiled. "So forget what I said about being popular and cool." I shrugged. "Who knows? Maybe surviving middle school means just being yourself."

Wait a sec. Was I channeling Ella or what? That sounded like something she'd say, like the advice she'd given me about being true to myself. I think I figured out what that meant. I even sent Ella a quick text to tell her.

Mia Lee: Be true to ME! I get it now. Thx 4 the advice.

Ella Lee: What????

Never mind. I'd explain later.

"Rory," Daniela said, "did we just miss something here?"

"I think so," Rory said.

Caroline and I both smiled when I said, "It's a long story about a couple of second grade cowgirls."

"You have to tell us sometime," Rory said.

"We will," I promised.

But it would have to wait because Mr. Postin stood at the front of the room again. He cleared his throat and said, "Attention please! I have some exciting news to share with you all."

Everybody stopped talking. It was like that pin-drop thing from this morning all over again.

"Let's have a round of applause for our new Video Production Club president, Blake Lyle." Mr. Postin motioned for Blake to stand up. When Blake did so, everyone clapped and cheered.

I even shouted, "Way to go, Blake!" And I meant it. His video really was awesome, with top-notch graphics.

"I'm sorry you didn't win, Mia," Caroline said.

"It's okay." And hey, I meant that, too. "I mean, I'm still in the club. But since I'm not president, I just have more time to hang out with you guys."

"Definitely," Rory said.

"I've been thinking," I said, "maybe we could even create more cartoons."

Then we started talking all at once about some different ideas.

"Mia, that's exactly what I'd like to talk to you about." Mrs. Wheatley, our school librarian, came over. "As you may know, I was on the video presentation committee, so I had the opportunity to view your work," she said. "And I have to be honest, I enjoyed your video the most."

"You did?"

Mrs. Wheatley nodded. "After twenty-four years of being a librarian, I know a good story when I hear one. Or in this case, when I *see* one." She smiled. "So I'd like to talk to you about featuring your video on the school website."

"The school website?" I said. "But why?"

"Well, if you are okay with it," Mrs. Wheatley continued, "your video will go on the front page of the T-W Middle School website for all the students and parents to see as part of our 'Student Work Showcase.' That way, whenever students want to check their e-mail, or parents want to check their child's grades, they'll be able to see your video, too. How does that sound?"

"Yes! I mean, sure. It sounds great. That's so many people," I said. Seriously, I was excited that people in this room would know more about my story. Now the whole school would, too, even Marcus McBully.

Mrs. Wheatley held up her hands. "There's more. There aren't too many movies or books where a main character has a disability, so I think your story is very unique. I'd like to contact other librarians at other schools across the state about possibly sharing your video as a learning tool with their classes as well." She smiled again. "You see, this isn't just your story."

"It isn't?"

"Oh no, Mia. There are so many boys and girls with various disabilities. You were brave enough to share your story. And I think it will help others to see that they are normal, too, just like you."

Wow! I might get to share my story with lots of kids. If they understood, it may stop a lot of the stares and whispers. It wouldn't be just for me but also for other kids with disabilities. And to think, it all started with Ms. Randells's English essay assignment. Wait until I tell Ella.

As if Ella had read my mind, a text pinged on my phone.

Ella Lee: Dude! I saw your campaign video! It's awesome!

Mia Lee: Thanx! I can't believe you already watched it.

Ella Lee: Not just me! You already have 1,000 likes on it. Amazing! Proud to be your sister.

I slumped back in my chair. I could hardly believe it. I must have looked shocked because Rory, Daniela, and Caroline all crowded around me, trying to figure out what was going on.

Caroline saw the text first. "One thousand likes—Mrs. Wheatley hasn't even posted it to the school website yet," she gasped. "This is going to be huge."

"Your videos are going to be famous," Rory jumped in, making this big sweeping motion with both hands. "Like across the country even."

"*You'll* be famous, Mia," Daniela said. "Before you know it, there'll be books and movies about you."

Mrs. Wheatley laughed. "Congrats, girls. Let's not get ahead of ourselves now," she said before she walked away. "I'll let you know when I talk to other librarians about featuring your video in their schools, Mia."

"Thanks, Mrs. Wheatley," I called after her.

Mrs. Wheatley had said to slow down, but it didn't stop the other girls. They weren't finished daydreaming.

"Action figures!" Caroline squealed. "When you have your own action figure, that's when you know you're really famous, Mia."

I just shook my head.

"Seriously, Mia," Caroline said. "How many people do you know who have their own action figure?"

"Um, let's see. Exactly"—I pretended to count—"none."

"See? Only famous people, that's what I'm talking about," Caroline said.

I laughed. "Well, if I ever have my own action figures, there'll be four in a box."

"Why four?" Rory asked.

I pointed to myself. "One." Then I pointed at each of them. "Two, three, and four." I smiled. "Hey, I've gotta have you guys to hang out with. Being an action figure all by myself wouldn't be any fun."

We all laughed. Then Caroline put her hand in the middle. "Best friends," she said.

I put my hand in. "Forever."

Rory and Daniela put their hands in, and they both said, "Forever," as well. On the count of three, we raised our hands in the air. Then we laughed all over again.

VP Club, sharing my story with the rest of the world, sharing my world with my three best friends...Maybe wheeling through middle school wouldn't be so bad after all.

ACKNOWLEDGMENTS

This book would not have been possible without the help of our agent, Clelia Gore, who believed in us from the very beginning, and helped us every step of the way.

We'd like to thank Amy Cobb, whose writing and editing skills brought the story we wanted to tell to life. Through all the rounds of editing, your patience and faith in our mission moved us tremendously. Thank you for helping us share Mia Lee and her story with the world.

We'd also like to thank Brittany R. Jacobs, our illustrator. Thanks to you, Mia looks exactly the way we (and so many others who supported this book) pictured her.

Thanks to all of our Kickstarter backers: Sherry Kempf, Sarah Tays, David Jacques, Martina Robinson, hmspepper, Rebecca R, Laura Minges, Jodi McCarthy, Jessica R. Kratz, Janis Totham-Davis, Annette Brooker-Grogan, Kat Simmonds, Lonny K Johnson, Andrew Erlanson & Zxy Atiywarii, Paul Puttlitz, Lisa Norris, David A. Katz, Cathleen Wolff, Helen Luk, Stacy Stone, Lyn, Paul Beery and Miriram K Schwartz.

Thank you to Rebecca Cokley and Maria Town, our advisors in DC, for helping us introduce Mia to the world and get her in the hands of the Hidden Army community.

To all 150,000 signers of our American Girl petition on Change.org on New Year's Eve, 2013, for a Girl of the Year who had a disability, we hope we made you proud.

To Mom & Dad, thank you for supporting us every step of the way. Melissa promises she'll try to eat more vegetables.

To all the kids with disabilities out there, keep being awesome.

ABOUT THE AUTHORS

Melissa and Eva Shang are two sisters who started a viral online petition in December 2013 in support of asking The Pleasant Company, makers of the American Girl dolls, to release a Girl of the Year doll with a disability. The petition gained over 140,000 signatures and was featured in all major news outlets, from BuzzFeed to People Magazine to the International Business Times. The Pleasant Company acknowledged the Shang sisters' petition, but could not commit to their request. That's when Melissa and Eva decided to take matters into their own hands and write their own book featuring a heroine with a disability, with the hopes of one day also having a doll to go along with it.

Melissa, who has Charcot-Marie-Tooth disease, a form of muscular dystrophy, is a seventh-grader at Gibbons Middle School in Westborough, Massachusetts. Since the petition went viral, Melissa has gone on to become a young disability advocate. She has given a TEDx talk, spoke at the United Nations, and introduced Malala Yousafzai at the National Constitutional Center.

Eva is a twenty-year-old student at Harvard University and is Melissa' #1 fan. An entrepreneur backed by Y Combinator and the Thiel Foundation, she is the co-found of Legalist, a legal analytics startup that tracks court cases for lawyers.

You can learn more about Melissa and Eva at www.melissashang.com and www.evashang.com.

Made in the USA
San Bernardino, CA
20 September 2017